TWIST OF FATE

A DCI HARRY MCNEIL NOVEL

JOHN CARSON

DCI SEAN BRACKEN SERIES

MAX DOYLE SERIES

Final Steps
Code Red
The October Project

SCOTT MARSHALL SERIES

Old Habits

TWIST OF FATE

Created with Vellum

ONE

She lay in the darkness, barely awake. The time had come for her to move on and she was prepared for it. Her time on earth had been good, a life well-lived, if not exactly according to the rules.

There was a morphine pump hooked up to her, but she didn't feel it, only the effect of it.

The door to the room opened, and a man walked in.

'Is that you, son?' she said, her words a hoarse whisper.

The doctor walked forward and smiled at her. 'It's the priest, Helen. You asked me to call him. He's here now.'

A man dressed in the garb stood behind him, clutching a Bible.

A tear rolled down one of her cheeks, and she smiled as best as she could. 'It's time,' she said, feeling relief at seeing the man standing next to the doctor.

The doctor nodded. 'It is. I'll leave you now.' He turned and opened the door. A nurse walked by and the woman could hear a raised voice from somewhere else in the hospital.

The doctor closed the door behind him. The priest stepped forward, smiled and gently placed a hand on hers. 'I'm here to help you move forward,' he said.

'I know. I want to hear your prayer before I go,' she whispered, feeling weaker by the second.

'I'm going to start the prayers now.'

She looked into the priest's eyes. 'I've sinned so much in my life, Father. I need to be forgiven.'

'That's why I'm here.'

She drifted off as the priest's words echoed around the stark room. He spoke in a quiet and even voice. This hospital was much smaller than Raigmore, and much quieter. Not deserted, but quiet enough for his words to be heard clearly.

He carried on as if she were sitting up, hanging on to his every word.

DCI Mike Holland felt tired as he pulled over onto the right-hand side of the street, an artic thundering past, rocking his car for a moment. The bastard had been up his arse for the past few miles, reminding him of that Steven Spielberg film *Duel* where the nutter chased Dennis Weaver in a truck.

He yawned as he got out of the car. Darkness had slowly come down and he couldn't remember where the transition between daylight and sunset had been. The drive from Glasgow had been long and boring. He'd ended up listening to some podcasts, true crime. Like he didn't get enough of that in real life.

He looked across at the Stag's Head hotel, with the promise of a pint of McEwan's, according to the lit sign. A pint would go down a treat right now, but one would lead to two and then another, and the tiredness would join the dance, and before long he'd be pished, and then one of the local johnnies would take great delight in locking him up and then all he'd worked for would be gone. He could hear a toilet being flushed, taking his pension with it.

Six months to go, he reminded himself. Six months to the day. September thirtieth would be the day he said goodbye to it all and he could relax. His sixtieth birthday. Christ, that had crept up on him.

He locked the car and took his phone out, wondering if the reception had got any better since he hit Golspie. He tried dialling the number once again and got the same answer: nothing. No reply, no mailbox.

He'd tried emailing again, sent letters, birthday and Christmas cards, but nothing. His trip up here was possibly going to be the last one, he knew that, but he had to try.

He walked into the chippie to get two fish suppers. He knew she liked that. If he turned up on her doorstep with a chippie, she might be more likely to let him come in.

He waited behind a young couple and ordered the suppers, then got back in his car. He wondered if that was the highlight of the couple's night: fish and chips, then back home to watch TV. Maybe a quick fumble up the lassie's sweater.

He was feeling apprehensive now. Christ, he'd fought hard men in bars, in the station when they'd decided to have a go, and out on the streets of Glasgow, but absolutely nothing had made him feel this way.

Meeting his mother again.

He drove off, the headlights cutting through the dark. He'd given the guesthouse owner a heads-up, telling her that he would be late but he was still coming.

Then he was in his mother's street, outside the little terraced house she had moved to from Dunfermline. *I want to feel peace again,* she had told him. *Get back to my roots.*

He had told her that it was a long way for his girls to come see her, but nothing had put her off. Now his girls were grown up, leading their own lives, and didn't have the time to come north for a visit. His mother's age and grasp of technology had prevented her from going on her phone and using WhatsApp. The girls weren't always around to call her, but when they had tried, they got no reply.

There were no lights on in the house. Maybe she was in bed already. He looked at the clock in the car: 7.57. Maybe she did go to bed early these days, but only a couple of years ago when he'd last visited, she'd told him she was a night owl and she stayed up late watching films on Netflix. Maybe it was bingo night somewhere. Would she go out and not leave a light on? Of course. This wasn't Glasgow. No gangs of wee hooded neds riding through Golspie. She was still very old, though, and some people couldn't help themselves.

He left the fish suppers on the passenger seat. The smell was making him feel hungry now, but he resisted the temptation to open one of the packets and get wired in.

He got out into the cold night air. Maybe it was his imagination, but it felt so much colder up here than down south. He climbed the couple of stone steps and knocked on the front door. There were porches attached to the front of the houses here, like somebody had thought about building a wee hut then thought that would be stupid so made it into an entryway instead. He knocked again, shoved his hands deeper into his overcoat pockets and watched his breath shoot into the air before going its own way.

He knocked again, harder this time.

'Here! What's all the bloody noise?!' a voice shouted from next door. Holland stepped back and peered round his mother's porch and saw an old man next door peering round his.

'Sorry for the noise. I'm here to see Helen.'

'At this time of night? Away ye go or I'm calling the polis.'

'I am the polis. But right now, I'm her son. Mike.'

The man squinted, sizing him up, looking like he

was expecting Holland to pull out a ski mask before coming over and pushing him into his house to rob him of the few possessions he owned.

'Mike, you say. She never mentioned any Mike.'

Oh God. 'I've only been here a few times before. You might have seen me.'

'A glaikit bastard like you? I would have remembered you, son.'

'Don't be sayin' that, Bill,' a female voice said. A woman, as yet unseen. Then she popped round behind Bill and stood looking at Holland, pulling her thick sweater tighter. Her hair was white and curly and was waiting for its nightly ritual of being bombarded with curlers, whether it wanted it or not.

'Mike, you say, son?' she said, smiling at him. There was a short distance between them, giving her time to shove the old man inside should Holland show any sign of taking out a butcher's knife.

'Aye. DCI Mike Holland, Police Scotland, Glasgow Division.' He looked back at Helen's living room window. *If you're in there and you've been woken up by the commotion, now's the time to show yourself.*

Nothing.

'We've only been here about six months. Helen's very nice, but she never mentioned you.' The smile, still there, ready at a moment's notice to turn into a snarl.

'We've...been estranged for over a year now. Something over nothing, but my mother's a wee bit stubborn. I thought it was time to bury the hatchet and come up here in person.'

The old woman, who still hadn't introduced herself, looked at her husband, before making eye contact with Holland. 'You have ID on you?'

Holland was amused for a moment, thinking they must have a proliferation of bogus gasmen coming round, but then felt guilty. If a stranger came to his mother's door, he would want her to be cautious too. But knowing Helen, she would invite the stranger in for a wee swally.

He fought down the bitterness. That wasn't why he was here. He took out his warrant card and held it out for the woman to see.

'I didn't catch your name,' he said, smiling.

'Don't tell him,' Bill said.

'Oh, hush now. Away and get the kettle on.'

Bill tutted. 'I've got a chainsaw, you know,' were his parting words as he went indoors. As it went, Holland had heard worse.

'It's for his hot-water bottle,' the woman explained, in case Holland thought he was being invited in for tea. 'The kettle, not the chainsaw. My name's Catherine Baxter.'

'Pleased to meet you, Catherine.' Holland put his warrant card away and had another quick glance at his mother's unlit living room, hidden somewhere behind the net curtains.

'Do you know if Helen's in?' Holland asked.

'Look, Mike, I'm sorry to have to tell you this, but your mother's very ill. She's been in the hospital for a few weeks.'

Holland felt a jolt inside, but like all the other times in his life, he fought it right away and focused. That had kept many a knife from going into his guts.

'Hospital? Raigmore?' He thought about the fifty-mile drive from Inverness to here, passing the hospital on the way up. He was quickly calculating how long it would take him to get back down if he drove like the arse of his car was on fire and the brakes were out.

His thoughts were cut short by Catherine talking.

'No, she's right here in Golspie. Lawson Memorial.'

'What's, er...what's wrong, do you know?'

'Has nobody told you?'

'I have an auntie and uncle, Helen's sister and

brother, but I've only ever met them twice. Once at a funeral. Long story.'

'She has cancer, son. They took her to Raigmore for the operation, but she was very ill. They transferred her up here.'

'I never knew,' Holland said, his voice low in the cold air. 'Thanks for telling me. I need to go and see her now.'

'Give her our best, Mike.'

Holland didn't hear the last part. He was rushing to his car. The smell of the fish suppers suddenly made him feel nauseous as he started it up. He was about to slam the car into reverse when he realised something.

He saw Catherine still standing there watching him and he wound the window down. 'Where is it?' he asked. 'The hospital?'

'On the main road leaving town on the way south. There's a sign. You go over the railway bridge and it's over on your right, set back from the road. You can't miss it.'

He nodded his thanks and reversed the car before shooting forward out of the small square and heading down to the main road south. The journey took him all of five minutes, his headlights catching the sign for the hospital just before the entrance.

The white building was lit up and he wondered which window his mother was behind, if she was even in the front of the building. He parked up, left the fish suppers where they were and rushed in. At reception, he was told to go up to the second floor, where a nurse would show him to his mother's room.

The hospital wasn't heaving like it might have been in Glasgow; there was more of a steady flow. A nurse sat behind the station at the head of the ward and he strode out of the lift straight towards her, warrant card in hand.

'DCI Mike Holland. I just learned my mother's here in the hospital. I drove up from Glasgow to see her.' He was about to include the part where he met Chainsaw Bill, which would have carried more weight if he'd actually *seen* the old man's weapon of choice. *Don't bring a knife to a chainsaw fight,* he imagined the old man saying. He skipped that part, taking a deep breath instead.

'Oh, right. She's in room 204. I'll get Claire to show you,' the nurse said.

Another young nurse was sitting close by at another part of the station, filling out paperwork. She looked round and smiled at him.

'Mrs Wardlaw's son?'

'Aye, that's me.'

'She never mentioned you.' Claire stood up, no inference edging her voice.

'We've been out of touch for a little while. I came up to make amends, and just found out she's in here. Nobody told me before tonight,' he said, looking at both of the women in turn.

'Well, you're here now, Mr Holland. Let's go and find the doctor.'

Claire stepped out from behind the station and he joined her in walking along the corridor. He wondered if she had wondered why he and his mother had different last names. Hopefully, she thought that Helen had got remarried and changed her name, rather than given her son away when he was six weeks old and had the adoptive parents change his name.

If she was thinking any such thought, she gave no indication of it.

They approached the room and Holland saw the door was open. There was a window next to the door, but the blinds had been dropped, cutting off the view of the inside. Claire stopped and knocked before entering.

A doctor was inside, standing next to a man in black. A priest, Holland saw when he followed Claire in.

'Excuse me, Dr Samuel, but this is Mrs Wardlaw's son, Mike Holland.'

The men both turned round to look at him.

'I'm sorry to tell you, Mr Holland, that your mother passed away half an hour ago. My condolences,' Samuel said. He was an older bloke and had probably told thousands of people their loved one had departed this earth before carrying on with his own life.

Holland nodded, and Samuel left. Claire stepped closer to him now.

'I'm so sorry, Mike,' she said in a low voice, as if she had been elevated to friend status, which opened the door to her calling him by his first name.

'Thank you.'

'I'll be along at the nurses' station if you need me.'

He nodded as the young woman left the room.

'I'm sorry for your loss, Mr Holland,' the priest said, and Holland nodded to him, but his eyes were focused on the woman's face. The crisp white sheet had been pulled up to her chin. Her face was pale, her heart now stopped from sending any blood to her extremities. Her hair looked greyer than he remembered, but maybe that was just his imagination. It was in a different style and cut, much shorter than it had been the last time he saw her.

'She's in a better place now, Mike. May I call you Mike?'

How could he say no? 'Of course.' He held out his hand and the priest gripped it, shaking it a couple of times.

'I'm Father Dan O'Brian.'

Holland let go of the man's hand. He was taller than Holland, with a nice set of teeth and a good head of hair. He looked younger, but Holland knew looks could be deceiving.

'I hope my mother was at peace when she passed' he said, turning his attention back to his mother.

'She was. She asked me to read her prayers. She knew it was time to go and wanted to feel like there was no more worry in her life. She left with peace in her heart, Mike. She knew she was going to a better place.'

He nodded before looking back at the priest. 'You knew her well, I take it?'

'I did. She was a wonderful woman. She was proud of you. She spoke fondly of you, Mike. Even in the past few days as her health deteriorated, she would speak of you.'

'Really? Did she say what a complete bastard I am?'

O'Brian smiled. 'The exact opposite. She told me stories of when you were born and how she loved you and it broke her heart to give you away, but back then it wasn't the done thing, having a baby out of wedlock. She loved you more than anything, Mike. You coming back into her life was the best day of her life. And your girls being born, making her a grand-mother, well, that was the icing on the cake.'

Holland swallowed. He felt the emotional turmoil starting to ascend in his guts, but he had long ago learned how to control his emotions. It was a skill that you learned quickly after attending scenes where victims had met a demise that was not a peaceful one like his mother had been afforded.

The stupid argument they'd had could have been avoided if he'd just lied to her. Or at the very least omitted the truth. But he had been honest with her: he'd done the Ancestry DNA thing and had connected with his two half-brothers.

Helen had exploded, asking him how he could have done that. He had hurt her badly, she said, and if he had loved her, he wouldn't have done that.

But Hugh and Walter Nichol had agreed to meet Holland, and he had felt at ease with them. The youngest brother, Hugh, had reservations, though. He hadn't known about Holland, but Walter had found out when he was an older teenager and had known they'd had a brother for all these years.

Holland had met Walter several times after that but hadn't met Hugh again. Walter had told Holland that Hugh would come round and things would go okay. *Just give it time,* he said.

He wasn't so sure about Helen.

'She loved my girls so much,' Holland said, looking O'Brian in the eyes.

The priest smiled and looked at him. 'I know she did. She told me about them.' He clapped a large hand on Holland's shoulder. 'She never stopped loving them, nor your wife or you. Helen loved having a family.'

O'Brian took his hand back as Holland once more looked at the old woman in the bed. The woman he hadn't got to say goodbye to. Who he hadn't spoken to in a long time. Who he never got to tell one more time that he loved her.

It was at this time that he finally caved in and allowed the sobbing to take hold of him.

O'Brian stepped forward and put an arm around the detective's shoulders.

Holland didn't object.

TWO

Old Mrs Crawford waved the cigarette smoke away from the frying pan and looked at the clock in the kitchen again. Five past nine. The pair of bastards were late. Again.

'Did you call them?' she asked her husband, a round, chubby man who was seated at their kitchen table, reading a newspaper.

'I did,' he answered after turning the page.

'Buy a guesthouse, they said. It'll be fun, they said.' Mrs Crawford shook her head and took one last sook of the cigarette before stubbing it out in the ashtray next to the cooker. She looked at her husband and wondered what she had done in her early life to deserve being lumped with this poor excuse for a human being.

'It's nearly time to shut the kitchen down,' she said, coaxing a couple of sausages round the frying pan.

'What?' Mr Crawford said, managing to peer over the top of the paper.

'Go and give them a knock.'

'Who?'

'Who do you think? The honeymoon couple. Remember, that was us, many moons ago.'

Mr Crawford made a sound like he was bringing his breakfast back up. 'My gout's acting up. Can you go? I'll keep an eye on the scran.'

Mrs Crawford took her pinny off and tossed it onto the counter before looking at her husband and shaking her head, wondering if the insurance money would be enough to keep her going after her husband's sudden demise.

'Well, come and keep an eye on the food. I don't want it burned.'

'Och.' He folded his paper and got up to take over fry-up duties while she left the kitchen and trudged upstairs. Just as well the honeymoon suite was on the first floor, although 'honeymoon suite' was pushing it a bit. The bathroom was a wee bit bigger and the mattress had springs in it that you couldn't feel. The headboard still rattled off the wall, but that was more a badge of honour than a one-star on Tripadvisor.

She stood in front of the bedroom door, listening. Her endearing other half said it was eavesdropping, but she preferred to call it being a diligent landlady. There was no headboard thumping off the wall, no sounds suggesting that the bride was being murdered or was repetitively calling on a higher power (with the noises she had been making the past few nights, it might be hard to tell the difference).

She knocked on the door and there was a quick bark from inside. These honeymooners weren't first-timers, but in their early forties. So they were on honeymoon with their dog.

Mrs Crawford envied them; she wouldn't mind starting over again. Maybe get herself a nice toy boy, somebody from a warm country, like Morocco or Tunisia. She'd read about young guys from there wanting older women, but it was hard to find one who didn't just want a British passport. Still, having some fun for a little while was better than having none. Mr Crawford's idea of being adventurous was taking his boots off first.

She heard muffled voices, like the man was

telling the woman to put the bathroom toiletry samplers back, that it was too early to nick them, then the bedroom door was unlocked.

Ken Abercorn was a thin man with a weedy moustache. He wore a polo shirt designed for a man half his age, with jeans and trainers that looked like they'd been mugged off a tramp. They were also a brand that suggested that he was still at the 'trying to impress the bride' stage. He clearly didn't have money or else he wouldn't give a toss, and the bride wouldn't be complaining now that she had access to his dosh.

'Mrs Crawford,' he said. 'Good morning.'

'Good morning. I came up to see if you still wanted breakfast? It's past nine o'clock and the kitchen closes at nine normally.'

'Oh. The chef in a hurry to get away?'

I'm the chef, cheeky bastard. 'Busy day ahead. I'll close up in five minutes, so if you still want it, it will be there, but it'll get cold.'

'I still want it,' a voice said from within the room, at a volume usually reserved for somebody who's pished and has long ago lost all control of their bodily functions. This was followed by a giggle.

Oh God. Mrs Crawford tried not to contort her

face, but it was hard. She settled for gritting her teeth and narrowing her eyes.

'How's Skipper this morning?' she asked, wondering how the little dog could hold its bladder for so long without pishing on the furniture.

'Oh, he's fine.' Ken turned to look in the room and saw Skipper dragging his arse along the carpet, back legs sticking up in the air, heading in his direction. He gasped and hopped both legs over a bit to narrow the gap between the door and the frame, but the dog turned round and headed back in the direction it had come from.

'We'll be right down. Sorry to have held you up, and don't worry, I'll add a little something for your trouble.' He smiled at her, stretching the moustache out sideways.

'Okay then,' Mrs Crawford said, trying to look past the door, but Ken closed it gently before she could clap eyes on the skid marks the dog was leaving on the shag pile.

She hustled back down the stairs, wondering if she would get away with dropping fag ash on their breakfast, and went into the kitchen to find her husband snaffling one of the sausages.

'For God's sake,' she said.

'What? I was hungry.'

'You could have made toast, fat bastard.'

'Oh, charming, that is,' he said, going back to his table and picking up his paper.

Mrs Crawford could have sworn a piece of bacon had gone AWOL too. *Fuck's sake.* Luckily, Ken Abercorn was skinny enough that he looked like he wouldn't make it through the rest of the honeymoon, that whatever his affliction was it would take him in his sleep before he'd had a chance to pull the new Mrs Abercorn's nightie back down. He ate like a bird, and Mrs Crawford wanted to tell him he should shovel more down to keep his energy levels up.

She scooped the food onto the plates and dashed through to the dining room. She was pleasantly surprised to see her husband had put the toast out already and had topped up the jug of orange juice.

She heard feet thumping on the stairs like they were five and getting ready for school.

'Good morning, Mrs Crawford,' the new wife said, grinning from ear to ear.

'Good morning. I just served your breakfast.'

'Very kind. Sorry about the tardiness. We were up late last night.' Susan Abercorn put a hand at the side of her mouth and leaned in conspiratorially. 'If you know what I mean.'

'Oh yes, my husband and I often stay up late watching Netflix.'

'Oh no, I didn't mean that –' Susan started to say, but her husband nudged her.

She turned to look at him.

'Food's getting cold,' he said. He was holding on to Skipper's lead and the little brown dog looked up at him as if to say, *Hurry up, ya twat, I'm touching fur here.*

'I'll take him out to the street and let him do his business, then I'll be right back.'

Mrs Crawford watched him go out the front door with the little Border Terrier, while his bride walked back to the dining room. She was a skinny bitch too and would probably eat a slice of bacon at most. The cooked breakfast was wasted on her, but they'd paid for it, so they could stand and lick the dining room windows for breakfast for all Mrs Crawford cared, so long as she got her money.

The groom was back in suspiciously quickly, like Skipper's bladder had protested at the distance the dog would have to walk to the main road and had let fly on her flowers instead. If brown patches appeared on her lawn, she wouldn't have to look far to figure out why.

She went through to her private quarters, where

Mr Crawford was back in his chair, drinking more coffee, and was now halfway through the paper.

'You know, we should have a second honeymoon,' she suggested to him.

He looked at her. 'We didn't have a first honeymoon.'

'Yes, we did. It wasn't my first choice of a weekend in Paris, but we had a good time.'

'Your mother's caravan in Berwick was hardly a honeymoon. Especially since she turned up the next day and stayed for the rest of the week.'

'That's why we should have a second honeymoon. A real one this time.'

'And who would look after this place?' he asked.

'Gina can come in and stay for a week. She does a lot round here as it is, and we could get somebody in to help her.'

'Get somebody in to rake about in our belongings more like,' he said, holding the paper up higher now.

Mrs Crawford was in her late forties. Plenty of life left in her, she reckoned. If skinny malinky could get a second husband at her age, then there was hope for her. She wondered if the new bride had killed her first husband, and if she asked her and the answer was yes, would she give her some tips?

'I nearly gagged on that sausage,' Susan Abercorn said as her husband closed the driver's door of their car and started the engine.

'I aim to please,' Ken Abercorn replied, his weedy moustache once again doing its dance across his face. Skipper barked from the back seat.

'Time and place, Ken dear,' Susan said, giving his thigh a squeeze, before turning round and making smooching noises to the dog. Skipper stepped up and licked her nose.

'Mummy loves her wittle puppy, doesn't she? Yes, she does. Yes, she does.' The dog barked and attempted to dislodge his tail by beating it from side to side even faster.

Then she sat forward again and put her seatbelt on. Ken thought that his new wife had conveniently forgotten that Skipper had given himself a quick bath with that same tongue shortly after coming in first place in the bum-dragging contest, although there were no other rivals in that particular race.

'Do you know the way?' she asked as he gingerly drove the car down the incline of the small car park towards St John's Road. They lived on the outskirts of Inverness, and although both of them had been down to the capital at one time or another, they hadn't been down together.

He looked both ways, disappointed to see that the traffic here was a lot worse than in the town where they lived. It had been Susan's idea to honeymoon down here, despite his protestations. He had given her subtle clues as to his feelings on the subject, but all of them had washed over her head. His last and futile attempt to change her mind had been to suggest Dundee, which had resulted in a screwed-up face and a suggestion for where he could shove that idea, a place where his urologist might find it on his next prostate exam.

No, dear, I think Edinburgh would be the best place, she had said in that passive-aggressive way she had.

So Edinburgh it was. But on the outskirts. *I'm putting my foot down on that one,* he had told her in as firm a voice as he dare muster. *The city centre looks like it could have been designed by a monkey.*

'Oh, for fuck's sake!' he shouted as a cyclist thwarted his attempt to cross the road.

'Dear oh dear, we don't seem to be putting our homework to good use now, do we?' Susan said, tutting her disapproval.

Ken had forgot to mention to Susan when they had started dating that he was a different man behind the wheel of a car. It brought his inner road-rage bastard out. After the first time, Susan had looked at him like he had been hiding a hammer under his seat. After he had proposed, she had made him go see a therapist or else he was toast.

He had gone to see some old boy who had bleated on and on, blah fucking blah, and Ken had told him he no longer felt the need to shout and swear behind the wheel, but he was willing to tell him anything at that point just so he didn't have to go back and run the bastard over with his car.

'Sorry, dear. Little slip. My therapist said it might happen.' *Especially if you insist on going to fucking Edinburgh for our honeymoon.*

'Don't let it happen again, Ken. Skipper doesn't like it.'

'I won't, my love.' *Jesus.* Skipper was used to his swearing by now, because the dog was his. They both used to sit on the couch, watching TV and eating popcorn, Ken shouting 'What a load of shite!' whenever he wasn't satisfied with a show. Skipper would bark along in unison, and alternate between growling at some paedo TV presenter and chomping on popcorn.

Then Susan came into Ken's life and the swearing at the TV, eating popcorn on the couch and sitting around in his Y-fronts all went out the window.

Finally, Ken got out of the car park, not because there was a gap but because he *created* a gap, sandwiching himself in between an airport bus and a tipper truck, the latter driver leaning on the horn and shouting out the window, using the same words Ken used to use. He looked over to his wife and saw she had closed her eyes and was saying a little prayer to herself. He hadn't realised she was so religious.

'I think I peed a little,' she said to nobody in particular. He assumed it was the dog, as he himself couldn't give a flying fuck. If he'd said that out loud, he would have had to say *flying squirrel*, which really didn't have the same ring to it.

He got onto the bypass after gripping the wheel so hard he swore it felt loose now. His wife was taking back-seat driving to a whole new level by shouting out the instructions her phone was giving her on how to find Borthwick Castle. He took the wrong turn twice and was berated twice, his new bride suggesting that maybe Ken was a borderline window licker and had all the driving skills of a man who was already dead.

There was a period where the lack of conversation suited Ken just fine. In his head, he was already wondering if it was too late to have the marriage dissolved, or whether they should just visit the Falls of Shin on the way back home and be done with it. Widower didn't sound too bad when it was said in a singles' club.

'It's round here,' Susan said and he got the distinct impression she was actually talking to the dog, expecting Skipper to pass on the message.

He turned the corner and then saw the sign: *Borthwick Caravan Park.*

So this is what we've driven all this way for? he thought to himself. *To visit an abandoned caravan park. Why would you want to go to Disneyland Paris when you can come here and break your kneecap falling through the floor of some old scrapper of a thing?*

'Is this it?' he asked, hoping that the infernal woman talking out of Susan's sat-nav app was wrong.

'Yes. What gave it away?'

He took a deep breath and blew it out onto the windscreen. 'Look, I know I act like I'm touched in the head when I'm driving sometimes, but I just feel antsy.'

'You said you would try harder when we were driving down here.'

'And I am.'

'After shouting at the tractor driver, calling him a...what was it again?'

'Do I have to repeat it?' Ken felt like he was walking into a trap.

'Yes. It will help you heal.'

'A baldy-headed, old, badger-shagging fuckwit.'

Susan shuddered. 'Now that's the last time I ever want to hear those words coming out of your mouth.'

'Agreed. Now, show me around this' – *godfor-saken* – 'place where you made some wonderful childhood memories.' He was starting to wish he'd borrowed a shovel from the landlady. Maybe a roll of plastic sheeting if she had any banging about. Nobody would find the new Mrs Abercorn in this fucking dump.

He imagined some people might have different memories of this place, like catching typhoid or something, but Susan had gone on – at length! – about the times she had spent here with her mum and gran and how she and her brother had spent many a happy hour playing here. Clearly after having had their anti-tetanus jags.

Now the campsite looked like it was a horror

movie set and he was half-expecting a man with a machete to jump out and create some new memories for Susan.

They got out of the car, Skipper starting to haul on his lead, sniffing along the ground like he was a bloodhound. Maybe they'd find a stash of cocaine, or even better, the proceeds from a bank robbery where the robbers had all died and wouldn't come looking for it –

'…gran.'

Ken hadn't realised he'd been smiling at the thought. It was one of his fantasies, finding a huge stash of money. That and running away with a stripper to Vegas.

'Why have you got that stupid grin on?' Susan asked. 'Did you hear anything I said?'

'I'm just so happy to be here with you, my love,' he lied.

'I said, I had some great times here with my gran.'

'That's nice.'

He rolled his eyes as they moved in through the old entrance, the gates rusty and open, like they had given up the ghost on ever securing the place again, and he turned up his nose at the thought of some animal excrement getting on his good shoes.

'You should have said it was like this so we could have worn wellies,' he said to his wife.

'I don't wear wellies, love; you should know that by now.'

Skipper was zigzagging around, his nose in overdrive, joined by his tail.

Susan pointed out the old sweetie kiosk, now with a detached roof and graffiti-covered walls. An old function hall that had seen better days and a few old caravans that had given themselves over to nature.

But Skipper was more interested in a caravan that sat further back from the rest. It was actually in the woods that bordered the property, surrounded by trees. How it had got there was a puzzle, until they saw the old, overgrown track.

It looked like it might have been shiny at one point in its life, but was now settling down to retirement by letting the moss and other green pieces of nature shove themselves up its arse.

The door was open, and the canopy of trees above it made the interior look dark.

'Come on, Skip, let's go back,' Ken said, and the dog displayed all he had learned at obedience school by ignoring him.

'He just wants to have a peek,' Susan said, smiling. 'And so do I, Ken. This is exactly the sort of caravan we stayed in.'

'Mouldy and manky?'

'Don't be cheeky,' she said, and Ken could practically see her screaming inside as she gritted her teeth. He thought she might only have one nerve left and he was rubbing on it now.

They walked up the track, getting closer to the caravan, and Ken could smell the stink before they even got close to the door. Skipper got closer and stopped for a pee, before standing and looking at the open door, growling at it.

'Smells like something shat itself,' Ken said, turning his nose up.

'Language,' Susan said, giving him the side eye, like she had the time she'd introduced him to her best friend in the pub and the woman had spilled a drink over his crotch. 'Fucking clumsy cunt,' he'd admonished, jumping up out of his chair, and both Susan and the friend had opened their mouths in unison, neither of them finding a reply.

Ken had walked to the bathroom with the words 'He's not the one for you' ringing in his ears.

Now this was the same thing, minus the friend.

'It does smell a bit, but that's the smell of the country,' Susan said.

Ken was about to gag. He'd been in public toilets that hadn't smelled as bad as this, and that was saying something.

Skipper had no such reservations and hopped aboard the Shitehouse Express with an enthusiasm that apparently knew no bounds. Ken let the extendable lead do its thing and the dog disappeared out of sight, growling. Then Skipper started barking.

'God, what if there's somebody in there?' Susan said.

Get your fanny in there and check on Skipper then. 'Who in their right mind would want to go in there?'

'Well, I'll go in, will I?' She looked at him, not moving, using psychology, but his first wife had tried the same thing and it hadn't worked then either.

'You're the one who wanted to come and see the thing,' Ken protested, but just shook his head. Skipper had extended his lead as much as he was going to, and Ken pulled himself up and into the caravan, sure he felt a twang down in the honeymoon section, but he ignored it for now. If he had to fight through some sort of pain later that night, so be it.

As he stood up straight, the smell was even worse now that he was inside with it.

And then the source of Skipper's barking could be seen at the other end of the caravan.

'What's there?' Susan asked, still outside, but Ken didn't reply. He only turned round, pulling the dog behind him, and vomited over his new bride.

THREE

DCI Harry McNeil stopped at the gate to the old caravan park, where a female uniformed constable put up a hand. He wound his window down a fraction.

'DCI McNeil,' he said.

'Oh, right, sir,' she said, and stepped aside to let him through. He parked his bogging old pool car beside a police van and got out into the cold morning. The damp, spring air slapped him in the face as he reached in for his overcoat.

He slipped it on and locked his car. The caravan park looked like it had been dead for a long time, with weeds and bushes climbing over everything. He walked towards the far end.

He noted that DSup Calvin Stewart's car wasn't

here. His boss was very much hands-on and liked to be in the thick of the action, and he was conspicuous by his absence.

He saw a man and woman standing by another caravan, talking to a couple of uniforms. The woman seemed to have had something thrown over her and her hair looked a bit wet, as if she'd hurriedly washed it and had skipped the hairdryer bit.

'Witnesses,' DI Frank Miller said, coming across to him. He didn't have an overcoat on, and Harry half-expected the younger detective to take his jacket off and walk about wearing only a t-shirt. That seemed to be a thing amongst younger people.

'What were they doing out here?' Harry asked, giving the little dog a look. Its eyes followed him, like he'd nicked its ball or something.

'They're on honeymoon,' Miller answered.

Harry looked round quickly at the couple; they weren't youngsters. 'Honeymoon?' he said, looking back at Miller.

'Second time round for both of them,' Miller said. 'I spoke to them when I got here, but I'm sure you'll want to have a word yourself.'

'I will, after I've been inside the caravan.'

'Finbar O'Toole is in there right now, examining

the body, but unless the guy had a heart attack first, I would say the crossbow did the damage.'

'Where did the arrow get him exactly? I heard it was the head.'

'Indeed it was. Right in his forehead, and the tip exited the back of his skull. Somebody wasn't mucking about when they shot him.'

'Christ, this is a first for me,' Harry replied.

'Me too.'

DS Lillian O'Shea and DC Colin 'Elvis' Presley were coming out of the woods.

'Dare I ask?' Harry said.

'Just scoping out the rest of the camp,' Lillian said.

'We were, boss,' Elvis confirmed, in case his beamer contradicted Lillian's story.

'Let's get inside this hovel and see what's going on,' Harry said to Miller. They put on overshoes from the box that sat outside, then with gloves on, they climbed in. The first thing Harry was assaulted by was the smell. 'I was going to say I've smelled worse, but I can't think where.'

'The gents lavvy in Corstorphine springs to mind,' Miller said.

'What you get up to in your spare time is your business, Frank.'

'Oh no, it was just –'

Harry held up a hand. 'Let it go, son.'

He saw a figure dressed in a white protective suit in what would have been the living room area, which consisted of a semi-circular couch with a table in front of it. An overturned bottle of whisky was on the table, as were two glasses.

The figure turned to look at them, moving out of the way.

'Hello, Harry,' Finbar said.

'Hi, Fin. This is another fine mess you've gotten us into.' Harry didn't bother with the Oliver Hardy voice.

'It certainly is a mess. Have a look at this guy,' Finbar replied.

Harry saw for the first time what Miller had already clapped eyes on. A figure sat on the couch at the back window, which itself was opaque with dirt and whatever else Mother Nature had decided to throw at it. He was partly decomposed and had a haunted look on his face, like seeing the crossbow was the last thing he'd had on his mind.

'Do we have an ID for him?' Harry asked.

'Craig Smith. There was nothing in his pockets, but forensics managed to lift some prints. He has a record: assault.'

'How old was he?' Harry asked.

'Twenty-seven. His last known address was a place in Fife. There's no information about a next of kin.'

Harry nodded. 'I wonder who he pissed off enough to be shot in the head with a crossbow?' He looked at Miller. 'Maybe the assault victim?'

Miller nodded. 'Could be. The assault was on a woman.'

'Maybe an angry husband or boyfriend. Get Lillian to look into that angle.' Harry looked at Finbar. 'Can you have a wild guess how long he's been festering in here?'

'I'm going out on a limb, but I would say two to three weeks. If it had been summer, he would have been in an even worse condition.'

Harry looked at the man's sunken cheeks and eye sockets, the colour of the skin that looked like wax paper gone bad.

He nodded. 'I'm assuming that uniforms are checking local residences nearby?' he asked Miller.

'They are. But there are only scattered houses round here. Anybody could come and go and nobody would see them.'

They heard a noise coming from the door and someone stepped inside the caravan.

'God, I swear my knees are getting worse every year. My wife says I should go to the gym, but who has time for that?'

Harry, Miller and Finbar looked at the latest member of the Come and Look at the Dead Man Club. It felt like they should be charging admission.

Neil McGovern smiled at them. He was Frank Miller's father-in-law and head of the Scottish branch of the government witness protection programme.

'Hi, Neil,' Harry said.

'Morning, Neil,' Miller said.

'Morning, boys.' McGovern looked at Finbar before taking in the sight of the victim. 'Obviously, I didn't just drop in to have a coffee and a doughnut,' he said, stepping further into the caravan.

Harry looked puzzled for a second, then it clicked. 'He's one of yours.'

'He is indeed, Harry. When the request for identification was put through your system, his name was flagged in my system. That's why I'm here. No offence, Finbar, son, but I'm having him taken away for a private autopsy.' McGovern looked at Harry. 'I'll need any findings you get passed on to me. Any witness sightings, stuff like that. I'll also remind you all right now that you're now under the umbrella of the Official Secrets Act. Talking about it outside of this caravan will be punishable by having your balls wired up to a car battery. And I've had a news blackout put on this.' He smiled at the last bit.

'You want us gone from the investigation?' Harry said.

'On the contrary, I want you to lead it. However, I will also be involved. Your team are to share the details of any findings with me. You don't report it up the chain of command, like you sometimes have to. This stops on my desk. It will be a joint investigation, if you will.'

Harry nodded. 'Whatever you say.'

'I appreciate your cooperation,' McGovern said.

'We didn't really have a choice, though, did we?'

'Not in the slightest. I'm glad it's just you and Frank who are investigating. I've come across some stroppy bastards in my day. But they're not stroppy twice.'

'We'll get the ball rolling,' Miller said. 'I'll see if uniforms came up with any witnesses.'

'Good lad. One of my team will have a talk with the pair who found him.'

'Fair enough,' Harry said. 'We'll be in touch.'

'Catch you later, lads.'

Harry, Finbar and Miller left the smelly little

caravan and grouped outside well away from the van.

'That's a turn-up for the books,' Harry said.

'It's not going to look good for McGovern if that young guy was supposed to have been under his watch and he's ended up dead,' Finbar said.

They watched as another car pulled in and parked close to Miller's.

'The wife,' Miller said, and the three men turned to look at Kim Miller stepping out.

'Hi, honey,' she said, walking over to Miller. She stayed professional and skipped the peck on the cheek. 'Hi, Harry. Finbar.'

'Ma'am,' Finbar said.

'It's Kim, Finbar.'

'Right you are.'

'I see my dad's here,' she said, turning to nod at the black Range Rover that was parked further down, two men in black suits standing by the car in case any of the police officers suddenly turned rogue and had thoughts of nicking it.

'He's inside the executive suite,' Miller said, nodding to where the old caravan sat in amongst the trees.

'Bring your own welly boots, I see,' Kim said.

'There's a box of overshoes outside the van,' her husband told her.

'I wish my dad had given me a heads-up,' she said. 'I would have brought my little tub of mentholated rub for under my nose.' She looked at Miller. 'I don't suppose you have...?'

He shook his head. 'Sorry. We had to brave it as well.'

'Never mind. I had a light breakfast. Catch you later, boys.'

She headed towards the caravan.

'If you don't mind me saying, Frank,' Finbar said, 'you're punching above your weight there.'

'I was going to say "cheeky bastard", but I agree.'

Finbar laughed and walked away towards the mortuary van. 'Catch you later, guys.'

'Let's wrap this up, Frank,' Harry said. 'I'm sure Neil has everything in hand.' They walked over towards Harry's car.

FOUR

DCI Mike Holland woke up and wondered when his wife had redecorated their bedroom wall. The wallpaper was something his granny might have liked, with flowers and grass. There was a funny smell accompanying the visual assault. Not a fart-in-the-bed smell, but something...different.

Then his mother's face came at him, pale, waxy and dead.

The guesthouse. This wasn't his own bedroom, but the one he'd booked near his mother's house. The Fountain Inn. He lay staring at the ceiling for a little while, feeling a headache announce itself, then he remembered necking half a bottle of whisky the night before. With Dan O'Brian, the priest. By

Christ, that man could put the booze away, but then what else did he have in life?

Maybe his flock, ignorant bastard, he told himself.

They'd come back to the guesthouse, he and O'Brian, and one of the owners, Cheryl, said it was fine to use the dining room. She even heated up the fish suppers, and they washed them down with a few cans before getting wired into the whisky. The man of the house had joined them for a bit too.

'So sorry to hear about your mother passing,' Sam had said. 'Cheryl just told me.'

'Thanks,' Holland said.

'She was a fine woman. Always had a good word to say about people. We would often stand and have a wee natter in the butcher's. Such a pleasant woman. Gone too soon.' Sam had opened the whisky and poured some healthy measures. 'Here's to the memory of a good woman,' he said.

'To Helen,' O'Brian said.

'May you rest in peace, Ma,' Holland said.

And that had started the ball rolling, telling stories of Helen and how she worked in a volunteer place in Inverness, helping the homeless find a place to live, or young people who were having a hard time with life itself get back on the straight and narrow.

'You know the old saying, she would give you the shirt off her back?' Sam said. 'That was Helen. She would give you her last.'

They had clinked glasses.

'So what happens now, Mike?' Sam had asked.

Holland remembered taking a deep breath, feeling that he was about to lose it, but he had managed to maintain his composure. He looked at both of the men in turn before answering. 'You know, I've dealt with hundreds of families, guiding them through what happens after a death, but when it comes to my own family, I feel overwhelmed almost.'

'I can help you, Mike,' O'Brian said.

'Really?'

'Of course. I can be there when you go through Helen's house. Her things will have to be gone through, and other family members will have to be told. Do you want to do that tonight?'

'She has a brother and sister. My uncle and aunt.'

'If it makes it easier, I can call them for you.'

'Thanks, Dan, but I'll do it. Maybe you can be there. I'll call from Helen's house tomorrow. I don't have their details, but maybe she has an address book or something.'

'I'll still be around. I'm staying up the road in

Brora for a little while longer. I can come back down in the morning. Not too early, though, eh?' O'Brian smiled and winked and raised a glass. 'To Helen.'

'To Helen.'

The night had worn on, the whisky helping to dull the ache Holland felt inside. He didn't know when he'd eventually fallen into bed. Luckily, he had called his wife before he had got wired into the drink.

He got up at seven and showered before heading downstairs.

There was a mirror on the wall in the hallway and he stopped to have a look at himself. He looked like shite. Unshaven, bloodshot eyes – he looked like he was a tramp who'd found some decent clobber to wear.

He went into the dining room and sat at a table. Cheryl brought him a pot of coffee. 'My husband thinks you might be needing this,' she said, smiling at him. 'Sorry to hear about your mum.' She briefly put a hand on his shoulder.

'Thanks, Cheryl,' he replied, pouring a cup.

'Do you want anything cooked?'

He thought that he'd probably redesign the wall-paper pattern if he ate anything of substance, so he just shook his head. 'Still full from the fish supper last night, thanks. I'll just have toast.'

'I'll make you some.'

She left the room and Holland looked around. There was a young couple over by the window talking German, and an elderly couple over by the fireplace, in which logs were burning.

Holland thought back to the last time he'd actually talked to his mother on the phone, trying to focus on the sound of her voice. It was hard; she had been angry and bitter.

'They're my family too. I told you a long time ago that I wanted to meet them, but you put me off from finding them. Now I've done it and they want to meet.' That had been a year ago, and he'd since met his brothers, much to his mother's disapproval.

'You're just as stubborn as your father was!' she'd shouted down the phone.

His father, DCI Phil Nichol. Long dead. A man he had planned to go and visit, but he had listened to his mother describing what a bastard the old man had been and had held back. Nine years after he had met his mother, he had made up his mind to look up his father, only to find out he had died two years previously. He had mentally kicked himself.

He thought back to the conversations he had had

with her, or rather the poisonous vitriol that spewed out of her mouth when it came to his father.

'I was a young constable, and he was a DI. He made me feel special, like I was the only one in the world who mattered to him. It was only later, after I fell pregnant with you, that I found out that there were other special girls in his life. He hardly looked at me when I was big, and I got sent away to Edinburgh, where you were born.'

Holland hated to hear the stories of how she was sent to a convent for unmarried pregnant women, and how a couple from Glasgow had adopted him.

His upbringing hadn't been the worst, but it could have been a lot better. He had a roof over his head and food on the table and didn't get a belting, but his adoptive mother was very controlling.

They were both dead now, never having met or wanted to meet his biological mother.

'There you are, love,' Cheryl said, coming back with a plate of toast. 'Just shout if you want something cooked, otherwise I'll see you at dinnertime?'

'Yes, thanks.' He watched her walk away before bringing his phone out and looking at photos of his mother. He buttered the toast almost in a trance. It was soft and toasted to perfection, unlike the cremated remains he always made for himself.

He scrolled to one photo in particular. He had come up with his daughters a few years ago and a friend of Helen's had popped round and taken a photo of Holland with his mother and daughters standing on the front steps of her house.

He felt a sharpness inside, knowing that he was never going to see her standing there again.

He heard voices outside the dining room, and at first he thought it was more guests coming down for breakfast, but it wasn't. It was Dan O'Brian talking to Cheryl. When he came in, he was dressed in a jacket with his dog collar showing. He smiled at Holland.

'You mind if I join you?' the priest asked.

'Not at all.'

'If you don't mind me saying, Mike,' O'Brian said, pulling out a chair and plonking himself down, 'you look like something the cat threw up.'

'I can't argue with you there. How do you look like you've slept for the last twelve hours with no drink?'

'Some of us are lightweights, my friend. And when I say, some of us, I mean you. Me? I like a wee dram of an evening when I'm watching Netflix.'

'I can usually handle a lot more than that,' Holland said. He looked the priest in the eyes. 'Honest.'

O'Brian laughed. 'Of course you can.'

'A wee bit of toast, Father,' Cheryl said, popping another plate down on the table with another jug of coffee.

'That's very kind of you, Cheryl. Greatly appreciated.'

'Help yourself to anything you want.' She patted the priest on the shoulder before moving off to attend to the other guests.

'I wish I could get used to margarine or something, but you can't beat real butter,' O'Brian said as he buttered a slice of toast. 'Has the shock hit you yet?'

'It did this morning, to be honest. I wanted to pick up the phone and call her and I almost did, but then reality hit me in the face. I realised that I would never be able to do that again, and I could kick myself for not trying harder. I did try and call her long before now, but I should have tried more often.' Holland drank his coffee, which tasted better than anything he drank in Glasgow. Something about the water up here.

'You shouldn't blame yourself, Mike. What's in the past is in the past. There's nothing you can do to change it, but you can learn from it, just remember that.' O'Brian bit into the toast and made a noise of enjoyment. 'A moment on the lips and all that, but also remember that we're only here once. Enjoy yourself.'

'You're hardly a fat ba...guy, Dan. I mean, I have a wee paunch going on here, but you look like you could go ten rounds with Mike Tyson.'

O'Brian poured himself a coffee from the flask that Cheryl had put down and washed his toast down with it. 'Tyson wouldn't want to meet me in a fight. I have somebody on my side he wouldn't want to meet face to face. Besides, I don't like violence, so I'd chicken out.' He laughed and ate more toast.

Holland liked the man. He wished his own priest was of a younger generation, instead of sometimes getting on his high horse, all fire and brimstone.

'Did my mum come up to your church in Brora?' Holland asked. More toast, more coffee. Putting a lining on his stomach as if he was about to go out on the lash instead of recovering from one.

O'Brian smacked his lips and put his coffee cup down on the tablecloth, careful not to spill any and make a mess. 'Yes. Every Sunday without fail. I've been here covering for Father McLean for four months. Helen was in the audience as it were, front and centre. She was a volunteer at the church and had many friends. I got to know her very well.'

'Where's your home church?'

'Glenrothes. I was chosen because Father McLean asked for me personally. He and I go way back. I'll be sorry to leave here, whenever the good father gets himself back on his feet. I can't go into details, you understand.'

'I know. I just wondered how long you'd been a friend of my mother's. Talking of which, did she mention any other friends round here? People who we should contact to let them know of her passing?'

'One or two women around here that I know of. Plus you should call the volunteer centre in Inverness and let them know.'

'I will.'

O'Brian reached into a coat pocket and brought something out, depositing it on the table. It was a set of keys with a Lego Daffy Duck keyring. 'These are your mother's keys. I went along to the hospital before I came here and asked for them. I told them you and I are going to her house, so they let me have them. Now I'm passing them to you.'

Holland shook his head. 'I never even thought about it to be honest. I would have been standing at her front door like a lemon, not knowing how to get in.'

'Be a lemon no more, my friend. Besides, I'm

sure I could have given you a shimmy so you could break in. I mean, gain entry using your police powers.'

Holland smiled for a second. 'Helen would have found that funny.' He scooped up the keys and put them in his pocket.

Coffee and toast finished, they bumped into Cheryl on the way out. 'That was the best coffee and toast I've had,' O'Brian said. 'I thank you greatly. Sam is indeed a lucky man.'

'Oh, thank you, Father. Drop in anytime.'

'That's what's known as opening the floodgates,' O'Brian said with a chuckle.

Cheryl looked at Holland. 'You booked for a few days. Will you still be around after today?'

'I will. I want to see that my mother's estate is wrapped up, but estate is hardly the word. I mean, it's not as if she owned Dunrobin Castle.'

'Everybody has to be sent off properly, Mike.' She touched a hand to his arm.

He smiled at her. 'Thank you, Cheryl.'

The two men walked out into a cold, dreich morning, with rain drizzling down, hiding the monument of the great duke himself up on the hill somewhere above them.

'Fountain Road is named for the fountain in the

middle of the intersection up there,' O'Brian said, unlocking his car with the remote. 'Did you know that?'

'I did actually.'

'Nobody likes a show-off, Mike.' O'Brian grinned, looking at the detective over the roof of the car. 'Let me drive. I think I'm the more sober out of the two of us, although if we get stopped, you can maybe show your warrant card while I tell them they'll go to hell if they don't let us go.'

'It almost sounds like a joke: a policeman and a priest get stopped by the police. But I'm fine, I'll drive. It's just round the corner.' Holland got in the passenger seat of the medium-sized saloon, noticing it didn't stink of fish suppers or any bodily fluids like some of the pool cars did. God knows what some of those undercover bastards got up to.

It wasn't far from the B&B to Helen's house, just a hop, skip and maybe a wee bit of a jump. At least they didn't die in a fireball.

FIVE

'Craig Smith,' Elvis said. 'Hardly original for somebody in witness protection.'

'Anonymous by its very nature,' Harry said. The Firth of Forth looked cold and deadly as he looked across to it, like it was beckoning people into its embrace.

Too cold for that, fuckwit, Harry thought to himself. He hated going into the sea. He'd brought his son Chance here, to Burntisland, when he was a toddler. It had been summer then, the sun warm, making the day shimmer. A cold pint for the adults in the pub near the Links, a dip in the sea for the bairns. Not that Harry had gone for a pint. He didn't want to take his eyes off his son, and although the sea was full of people splashing about, just the thought of going into the water sent a shiver up his spine. The thought of jellyfish and other sea life and the occasional errant jobby touching his legs in the water made him want to puke.

He'd told Chance that he was allergic to seawater, and to this day he didn't feel guilty about that. It was a better alternative than shouting like a wee lassie with seaweed round his ankles.

His wife at the time had no such qualms and would paddle in the filth with wild abandon.

His vantage point now, high up in Burntisland, brought back memories of Chance when he was a boy. Sun, sea and seagulls dive-bombing on a poke of chips. Over the roofs of the houses further down the street, he could see a sliver of sea and some island that he didn't know the name of and wasn't really interested in finding out.

He looked at Elvis, who was still busy fannying about with the keys to the front door of the terraced house.

'Come on, son, what are you doing there? We're not trying to find our way into a secret passageway in a pyramid.'

'It's these bloody keys. Are you sure McGovern gave us the right ones?' Elvis stood up straight, looking flushed with his peeping Tom face on.

'He bloody well better have. I don't mind driving over here, but I'm not leaving empty handed. If we have to batter that door in, it's coming off the hinges.'

'By *we* you mean *me*.'

'No point in having a dog and barking yourself, son, is there?' Harry said.

Elvis didn't dignify the comment with a reply.

'Never mind. Just try the damn things again,' Harry said, looking around. There were two blocks of flats at the top of the road, and he wondered if there was anybody staring down at them, or some-body lying flat on their carpet wondering if they should just nash to the bathroom and start flushing. Or maybe they were all nice people who would invite them in for a cuppa and a chocolate Hobnob if he rapped on their door.

He thought they probably got a good view of the sea from up there. Poor bastards.

'Got it!' Elvis said.

'About bloody time.' Harry held out his hands for the keys and Elvis passed them over. 'Now let's see how this guy lived.'

They walked into the house, slipping on gloves. The lobby was narrow with a staircase in front and a living room on the right.

'Check through the back, Elvis.' Harry saw a

kitchen door straight ahead, and another door on the right.

'No problem.' Elvis walked along the hallway while Harry went into the living room.

The room was stuffy and there was a lingering odour of something that had been eaten a while back, or had died and crawled under the couch. He walked over to the window and turned the blinds so the dull light came marching in.

The TV was large but not 'compensating for a small penis' large. It didn't look that new either, and it sat on a cabinet that looked like it had been made by prisoners in the wood shop before they passed it along to the paint shop where somebody with the onset of cataracts had bravely thrown some paint in its direction. A DVD player sat on the shelf below the TV with a small stack of films to one side. Harry walked over and picked one up: *Hitman.* Other films were of an equally violent nature.

He tossed it back.

For a house belonging to a young man, it was remarkably tidy. No newspapers lying about; no open, unfinished cans of beer or detritus from the chippie, the result of a drunken night out. The same kind of things that Harry used to have lying about in his old flat.

There were no photos of anybody anywhere. No books, magazines or anything else that might tax the brain.

He walked out into the hall and heard Elvis banging about in the kitchen. 'You find any hidden contraband?' he shouted through.

'If I do, you'll be the first to know, boss.'

'I'm going upstairs.'

Harry started climbing the stairs, which weren't carpeted. The walls had woodchip wallpaper painted magnolia, the staple diet of council walls everywhere. He reached the landing and saw three doors. The one straight ahead led into the bathroom, strategically placed so that anybody who was in a rush could keep on running when they reached the top of the stairs, one hand fiddling with a belt, the other one blindly reaching out to slam the door, and hope they got to sit down before a trip to Marks and Spencer was called for.

The usual suspects were lined up on the sink: razor, shaving foam, toothbrush, toothpaste, hand soap pump. The sink was bone dry, which was to be expected from somebody who was miles away from home, sitting in a caravan with an arrow through his head.

The first bedroom was empty. The carpet looked

clean enough, and there were no marks from the feet of a bed, or an outline from a chest of drawers drawing its rectangular shape into the carpet. It was as if no furniture had ever graced the room with its presence.

The second room was different. If the first bedroom was the very epitome of cleanliness, the second room was its distant cousin, Manky Bastard. The cousin you didn't see very often growing up; the one you didn't like and couldn't give a toss about. He'd come round with your aunt and uncle every so often, and when he did, he would fart and laugh and wave his hand in front of his face and say 'Eat that, little fucker' before starting in on the toys, determined to break as many as he could before going home, and the ones he didn't break, he wanted to *take* home. When Mummy said no, he would tell you that you're a 'fucking dead man walking'.

This second bedroom was that cousin.

This was where the bachelor detritus resided. There was an old chest of drawers which looked like it had skipped the prison paint shop altogether and had gone straight for the shabby-chic look. Despite there being an actual place for clean clothes to live, whoever owned it – and there was no reason to believe somebody other than Smith had lived here – had decided it would be more fun to throw the laundry onto the floor. It was hard to tell which items had been laundered and which ones were waiting to play with the washing machine.

A single bed sat against the far wall, the covers and duvet looking like a tramp had got rid of them. There was a smell of stale sweat and some other bodily fluids that Harry didn't want to know about.

Beer cans, takeout food containers, newspapers – all the stuff he had expected to see downstairs was up here, like Smith had brought it all up in a wheel-barrow and attempted to make it look like modern art. The smell was worse in here, and Harry thought he should open a window but decided against it. He didn't want to be the one who had to come back in here and close it again. But then again, that was what Elvis was for.

Harry stepped over to the drawers, walking like he was making his way through a minefield, but instead of a mine, it would be a pair of dirty skids he'd be trampling all over.

He tried the top drawer. Nothing but underwear belonging to a man. Briefs rather than shorts.

Second drawer, polo shirts and t-shirts. Old receipts from shops, waiting to go in the shredder that sat in the corner. Maybe that was a requirement when you were in witness protection.

He opened another drawer to reveal some sweaters. He moved them aside and saw a bag of weed. He wasn't intimate with the ins and outs of being in witness protection, but he was pretty sure this wouldn't be on the list of approved pastimes.

Harry wondered whose head was going to roll for this cock-up.

He scanned the rest of the room and saw a pile of porno mags sticking out from under the bed.

Harry didn't know for sure, but he was willing to put money on it that the person who was supposed to be supervising Smith didn't pop in for a coffee very often. Had Smith been in this programme so long that he'd become boring for his handlers? Harry would need to ask McGovern.

He went back downstairs to find Elvis in the kitchen. Harry thought at first that the DC had made himself a coffee, but he was still raking about in the cupboards.

'Find anything?' Harry said in a loud voice, making Elvis jump.

'Jesus,' he said, whipping round like he'd just been caught with his hand in the biscuit tin. He shook his head. 'Nothing.'

'There's some weed in a bag in a drawer upstairs. He lived like an animal. His bedroom's a midden.'

'We should have somebody interview the family of the assault victim,' Elvis said.

'Way ahead of you. Frank's away to have a talk.'

'What about the family of the original victim?'

'We don't know who that was. I'm sure McGovern's got that covered.'

'Why let us run with the case?' Elvis said. 'McGovern has a big department.'

'We're low-key. If anybody sees us and asks, we're polis. Nobody will bat an eyelid. But if they see a bunch of suits wandering around, it might raise questions.'

'Makes sense.'

'Hello?'

Harry and Elvis both looked round at the sound of the voice. Harry walked out into the hallway to see an older woman standing in the lobby.

'Can I help you?' Harry asked.

'Who are you?' the woman asked. 'From the council?'

'Eh...aye. We're looking for the young man who lives here. He's behind in his rent.'

'That'll be young Craig. Och, he's no' a bad lad. Why can't you give him a break?'

Elvis stepped into the hall. 'We have,' he said. 'We came round to tell him that his rent arrears have been taken care of. Do you know where he is?'

'Can you take care of my arrears too?' The woman perked up, her slight stoop becoming less pronounced as her eyes lit up.

'We can certainly look into it.'

'I'm a couple of weeks behind.'

'Is that all?' Elvis said. 'Leave it with us. We'll have it taken care of.'

'Oh, you're such a good boy.' She covered one side of her mouth and nodded towards Harry and said, 'No' like him,' like he couldn't hear her.

'It might take a few days, but we'll get it taken care of,' Elvis said. 'However, we were going to help out one of Craig's friends as well. Have you seen him in here recently?'

'No, son. Craig really kept himself to himself. Except for that lassie who used to come round, but I haven't seen her for a while.'

'You wouldn't happen to know her name by any chance?' Harry looked at the old woman and thought she probably wouldn't know what day it was, never mind some strange lassie's name.

'Heather,' she said, surprising both detectives.

'He didn't introduce me, but I heard him shouting her name. She was angry at him for that.'

'How do you mean?' Elvis asked.

'Well, she was walking out to her car and she shouted, "Don't call me that anymore. I'm not Heather anymore. It's Amanda. Get that through your thick skull."'

'What did Craig say to that?' Harry asked.

'He said he would only ever think of her as Heather. He wouldn't call her Amanda.'

'Strange conversation,' Harry said. 'Was she here regularly?'

'I'm not finished, son.' She stood looking at them like a ratty old school teacher waiting for the little bastards to settle before carrying on with the lesson. 'She said, "Maybe I'll just call you Kevin then." She looked a little bit weird. One of those lassies who has earrings pierced through her nose and ears. God knows why they do that. And they get tattoos like they're bloody truck drivers.'

'Was she his girlfriend?' Harry asked.

'I don't know. She used to stay overnight sometimes, so she might have been. You know you get a discount on your council tax if you live alone? I bet he was taking them for a ride. But I didn't like her. My husband says I'm a nosy old cow, but I just like to keep my eyes peeled.' She held up a finger like they were going to interrupt her again. 'Being security conscious, I took a note of her car number plate. I'm going to give it to the polis.'

Harry looked at Elvis, then back at the woman. 'Could you give us the number plate?'

Pfff. 'I can't do that, son, as much as I'd like to.'

Harry looked at her; show his warrant card or keep up the pretence of being from the council? Then he had an idea.

'I understand. Now, what number did you say you lived at?'

'Twenty-six.'

'Okay, thanks.'

'You'll be able to take care of my arrears?'

'I'll certainly talk to the right people.'

'Aw, you're a braw lad.'

'Mrs...?'

'McPherson.'

'Thank you. Now, if you'll excuse us, we have to get back to the office.'

'No bother.'

Harry got Elvis to lock the door and they went back to their car.

'Take care of her arrears?' Harry said.

'I was in the moment.'

'Let's hope she's doolally and doesn't remember anything. If she does, act daft. Which shouldn't be that hard for you.'

'I feel I've been insulted.'

'You have been. I wasn't trying to hide that fact.'

'Fair enough.' Elvis started the car and drove away while Harry got on the phone.

'Alex?' His wife, who worked in Fife Division. 'I need a wee favour. There's a Mrs McPherson, lives at...'

SIX

'Did my mum get herself another car?' Mike Holland asked as O'Brian turned into the little dead-end street. He stopped, facing the house.

'Yes. That's it there. The old Vauxhall Astra. She used it to get to church and to do some shopping, but she wouldn't drive it down to Inverness. Too busy, she said. I'm sure the key is inside the house if you want to have a look in the car.'

Holland looked at the white car sitting along from Helen's front door, wondering when she had last driven it.

O'Brian sat staring out the windscreen before turning to Holland. 'You okay there, Mike?'

'Just thinking about my mother driving. Back when she lived in Dunfermline, we would go up to see her, and she would drive me and the girls to Asda to get something for lunch. My wife couldn't always make it, but I made sure the girls saw her often.' Holland turned to the priest. 'I made an effort, I really did. She's the one who chose to come here and leave us behind.'

'How old were you when you first met her?'

Holland thought about it for a second. 'Twenty-six.'

'And how old are you now? If you don't mind me asking.'

'Fifty-nine. I'll be sixty at the end of September.'

'Look at it this way: you had thirty-three years with her, Mike. You were with her longer than without. Yes, you missed out on being brought up by her, but she saw your girls growing up.'

Holland nodded before looking at the priest. 'Was she all there the last few months? Since you came up here?'

O'Brian said, 'Why, yes, she was. Very much so. She was sprightly too. But the cancer got hold of her. She told me she didn't want you to know. She just wanted to have the treatment and get better. If she didn't have long, then she wanted to be as well as possible so she could see you and the girls again.'

'You know, Dan, I can't understand why she

didn't tell me, her own son. Do you know if she told her brother and sister?'

O'Brian took in a breath and let it out. 'She told me she had told them both.'

'Christ.' Holland quickly looked at the other man. 'Sorry.'

'I heard nothing. The man upstairs, now I can't answer for him, but I'm sure he'll have it out with you when it's your turn.'

Holland gave a brief smile. 'You know, somebody said, if you go from New Year's Day to the following New Year's Day, you've lived through the day you're going to die. I wonder if Helen thought like that?'

'If she did, she didn't tell me, Mike. But let's go inside.'

They stepped out of the car, the drizzle still trying to soak them to the skin. Old man Baxter next door hadn't popped his head out, nor his wife. Maybe they wouldn't bother.

Holland took the keys out and picked one that looked like it would open the door, but it didn't. Finally, he got the right key and opened the front door into the little porch, and they walked into the hallway. The living room was on the right. O'Brian gently closed the front door behind him.

There was a smell of lingering polish and something that had been cooked a while ago, spicy and strong. It was cold in the house. The heating had obviously been turned off to save money while his mother was in the hospital.

Ghosts from visits past played in front of him. His daughters when they were little. His mother sitting in her favourite chair watching them, the inevitable cup of tea in her hand. To be replaced later on by a glass of wine.

When he had first met her in Hillend in Fife, it had been in the car park of the pub, which was located across the road from it. It had been as if he had known her forever. They had hugged and he had smiled. She was in her late forties back then, and he saw the resemblance of him in her face. It wouldn't grace the cover of any health or fitness magazine – the nose was too big for that – but it was his mother's face, and he had felt a love then that he had never felt before in his life.

'Is it how you last remembered it?' O'Brian said in a quiet voice.

Holland looked at him. 'Aye, pretty much the same.' He looked around at the little curio cabinet that sat next to the TV, his eyes searching for a certain item, but it wasn't there.

'Something wrong, friend?' O'Brian said.

Holland walked over to the cabinet, ducked and peered in. Then he stood up and looked at the priest. 'Strange. I gave her a little model of a Glasgow bus. It sat on that shelf right there. Now it's gone. I wonder why she moved it?'

O'Brian smiled at him. 'Always the detective, Mike. It was a wee bus. Maybe she let next door's grandchildren play with it. Maybe it's in another room.'

'She loved it. When she came down to my place, she had such a good time going around on the buses that I bought her one on eBay to remind her of the trip. We often talked about it. Maybe she put it back up on eBay. Or took a hammer to it.'

'I'm sure it's just been moved.'

Holland nodded and walked through to the kitchen at the back of the living room and looked around. It felt wrong, his being in here while she wasn't here, but it wasn't as if she was going to come walking back in and catch him doing something he shouldn't be.

The room was tidy. That was a trait his mother had: no dishes left in the sink, the countertop always clean, everything in its place. But right now, there were toast crumbs on the countertop in front of the toaster.

'This doesn't make sense,' Holland said.

'What's that?'

'This. My mother wouldn't have left a mess, especially since she was going into hospital.' He looked at O'Brian. 'Do you think somebody came in here?'

'Maybe the neighbours? Came in to water the plants?'

'Water the plants and have a bit of toast while they were at it? I can ask the couple next door, but the old boy didn't seem to be that friendly last night.'

'I can have a talk.'

'Thanks, Dan. Now, where would she have kept an address book? If she actually had one.'

'How about near her phone? I saw one sitting on the small side table by her chair in the living room.'

'Good idea.' Holland left the kitchen and walked over to her chair. The phone was right there, sitting on the answering machine. He hadn't noticed it before, the toy bus in the front of his mind. There was indeed a small address book next to the phone. He picked it up and first flipped to H, to see if his own name was there. It was. Not *son*, but *Mike Holland*.

He flipped through the book, finding his aunt's

name first. Davina Orville. She had obviously kept her married name after her divorce.

'I'm going to give her a call,' Holland said.

'I'll go and put the kettle on.' O'Brian left the room as Holland picked up the phone and dialled the number.

'Helen?' Davina said, answering on the third ring.

'It's Mike,' Holland answered.

There was a pause as if the daft old boot had forgotten who he was. 'Helen's son,' he said. If this had been years before in a public phone box, he would have heard the pips by now, telling him he needed to feed the box more money or he'd be cut off.

'I know who you are.'

Holland metaphorically bit his tongue. The last time he'd seen the old woman was at his grandfather's funeral. Very few words had been exchanged and they had gone their separate ways after the service.

'I just called to tell you that Helen died last night.'

Silence for a few moments, hanging in the air like a fog had descended on the room. Holland felt himself start to sweat as he waited for a reply, the room suddenly feeling claustrophobic.

'Everything okay, Mike?' O'Brian said, coming into the room. Apparently, he knew better than to watch a kettle as it attempted to boil the water.

Holland covered the mouthpiece as he looked at the priest. 'I don't think I'm on her Christmas card list.'

'*I know,*' his auntie said.

The words kicked him in the chest. 'How do you know? Did the hospital call?'

'*I just know, okay? Oh, and by the way, she left you fuck all. If it's her money you're after, then you're shit out of luck. Maybe you shouldn't have fallen out with her. Grubby little bastard. Why didn't you just stay out of her life?*' Her voice had risen to the point where she wasn't actually shouting but wasn't a kick in the arse off it.

'What about Uncle Dickie?'

'*It's Uncle Richard to you, little bastard. And he knows as well. So if you thought you were at the top of the tree, think again.*'

'Top of the tree? Really? How often did you get in touch with her? How often did you come up and see her?' Holland's cheeks were flushed now as if he'd just been running for a bus and the bastard had pulled away from the stop.

'More than you know. I spoke to her almost every day. I'm not the one who abandoned her and didn't communicate with her. You think about that, sonny.'

He hung the phone up and stared at the machine again for a few moments, as if not quite believing the words that had come out of it.

The last time he'd spoken to his mother, she had said she never heard from her brother and sister. Had they reached out to her when he and Helen were on what he liked to call a little sabbatical? Obviously, they had.

'My auntie just told me that she and my uncle already knew that Helen is dead,' Holland said. 'How would they know? Would the hospital have told them?'

'Maybe Helen left instructions with them, in case of emergencies. She never knew you were coming, remember? She would have had to name somebody as an emergency contact.'

Holland shook his head. 'I distinctly remember having a conversation with her about this very thing, years ago. If something happens, get your friend to call me, I said. Why didn't the friend call me to tell me she was ill?'

'Helen thought she was going to beat the cancer, Mike. She saw herself coming home and getting on with her life.'

'What was her friend's name again? Did she even tell you?'

The priest nodded. 'They both volunteered at the church. Maggie Quinn. She lives round the corner.'

Just then, the doorbell rang, and Holland went to open it. Standing at the front door was a woman.

'You must be Mike,' she said.

'I am. You have the advantage.'

'I'm Maggie Quinn. Helen's next-door neighbour called me and told me you were back.'

'We were literally just talking about you. Please come in.'

The woman huddled inside her coat as she stepped into the house. She looked to be in her fifties, so when she described Helen as being a friend, he assumed it was more of a neighbourly friend type of thing.

'Oh, hello, Father,' she said to O'Brian.

'Maggie. Glad to see you. Mike was about to call you.'

Maggie turned to look at Holland. 'Is everything alright with Helen?'

Holland took a deep breath before answering. 'Sorry to tell you, but she passed away last night.'

Maggie sucked in a breath and put a hand over her mouth.

'The kettle's just gone off,' O'Brian said. 'Tea or coffee?'

'Helen only drank tea. She didn't keep coffee.'

'Tea it is then,' he answered, disappearing into the kitchen.

Maggie sat down in what was once Helen's chair, now redundant. 'I can't believe it. I thought she would get better.' Tears were in the woman's eyes now.

'So did I,' Holland said, sitting on one of two chairs that were on opposite sides of a little dining table. 'I came here to make amends. You probably know we had a falling-out, something over nothing.'

'Aye, I did that.' Maggie produced a paper hanky from her pocket and wiped at her eyes. 'To be honest, I thought you were here to talk with your uncle.'

'Dick?'

'Aye. He was here for a few days. I saw him a couple of days ago. He was coming in here, so I thought Helen had suggested he live here while she was in hospital. I never spoke to him, but he took some boxes from here and put them in his car.'

Holland was puzzled, but then it all made sense. The missing bus. God knows what his uncle would want with that.

'Helen had a laptop. Do you know where she kept it?'

'I'm not sure. I know she kept it in a laptop bag. She would bring it to the church sometimes.'

O'Brian walked in with two mugs. 'Milk and a little bit of sugar for you, Maggie. I remember from the church meetings. Just milk for you, Mike. You can add sugar if you like.'

'Thanks,' Holland said, taking hold of the mug. He sipped the tea, which was surprisingly drinkable. He wasn't sure why he'd thought the priest wouldn't make a good cuppa; maybe he'd assumed men of the cloth only drank the hard stuff.

He put the mug down and followed O'Brian back into the kitchen, where he was fetching his own mug of tea.

'I don't suppose your mother was a fan of chocolate Hobnobs by any chance? She invited me in for a cuppa one day and she only had Rich Tea.'

Holland shook his head. 'Rich Tea,' he confirmed.

'No matter. Got to watch the old waistline, I suppose.'

They drank their tea and chatted, mostly about Helen, until Maggie took the finished mugs back to the kitchen.

'Listen, Father –'

'Dan.'

'Dan. I'm going to have a look around and see if I can find my mother's laptop.'

'You don't have to explain to me, my friend. You're her next of kin. If she didn't have a will, it will go to probate, but this is basically your stuff now. I'm sure nobody would mind you having a wee look through her things.'

'I'm not going to nick the silver. I just want to see if my uncle Dick had sticky fingers.'

'Gotcha.'

Holland started by looking through his mother's bedroom, giving it a going-over like he had barged in with a search warrant. Nothing. No sign of any computer, tablet or phone.

He went back to the living room, where O'Brian was giving Maggie a talk on the perils of gambling, like she was some kind of card shark.

'Did you find it?' he asked Holland.

'Nope.' Holland looked at Maggie. 'Do you know if my mother had an iPad or any other tablet?'

'No. She used her laptop to write emails and talk to the people she mentored in Inverness.'

Holland asked Maggie and O'Brian to help search for the laptop. He wanted to know if Helen had maybe tried to write to him before and hadn't managed to send the email. His mother had told him she always – without fail – wrote an email in a Word document first, because then she could edit any mistakes more easily and she could make the font bigger so it was easier for her to read. He needed to know if she had started any letters to him. It would ease his mind if she had. If she hadn't? Well, he would draw a line under it.

They searched everywhere they could think the laptop would be. Even in the laundry basket. If Helen had known she was going into hospital, maybe she'd made an effort to hide it rather than leave it lying about.

Then the house phone rang. Holland was in the bedroom with O'Brian and they looked at each other.

'Go and look, Mike. See who's calling.'

Holland nodded and walked through to the living room and looked at the caller display. It was a number he didn't recognise, but he picked it up and answered anyway.

'Hello?'

There was silence for a second and Holland wondered if there was anybody actually there.

'Hello?' he said again.

'You, ya wee bastard.'

Holland's adrenaline kicked in. He didn't recognise the voice, but it could only be one person: Uncle Richard.

His words were slurred and obviously alcohol-fuelled. Helen had told Holland about her brother's insatiable desire for a drink.

'Dick. I wondered when you would come crawling out of the woodwork.'

'Don't you fucking call me that. What the fuck are you doing back in her life?'

Holland thought for a moment that the old man didn't know about his sister's passing and he was about to tell him, but then the next lot of words came blasting through the phone.

'Did ye just wait until she popped her clogs before going raking through her stuff? She told me what a little fuck you were. And now you're there to pick through her stuff. Not even twenty-four hours deid and you're fucking ransacking her house! Copper or

no copper, I'm going to belt the living daylights out of you.'

Holland searched his memories of the old man and remembered he was almost ten years younger than Helen; that would make him seventy-two, give or take.

Words rattled through Holland's head, some sort of retort, some jibe that would cut through his uncle, but he rose above it. 'I'll tell you when and where the funeral will be. Come if you like, but if you're just going to cause trouble, stay away.'

'Don't you tell me what to do.'

'I don't suppose you'll need to come and see her off since you were already up here going through her stuff. And you accuse me of rifling?'

'I wasn't up at her house! How dare you.'

'Whatever. You'll find out about the funeral, but that's all the communication I want from you.'

'Fine by me.'

Holland hung up and ignored the phone as it rang again a few seconds later.

'That was rough,' O'Brian said, standing at the living room door.

'It was, Dan. He never liked me, and now my mother is gone, he didn't hold back.'

'On another note.' O'Brian brought a hand out from behind his back and held up a laptop.

'Where was it?'

'Maggie found it behind a radiator.' He handed it over and Holland nodded his thanks.

He took the laptop and sat at the small table as Maggie came back into the room. He opened it up, and between the top and bottom halves was a yellow Post-it note. He read the words scrawled on it: *Mike, I left this for you. Remember the first place we met and the year?* Hillend, 1989; a password any schoolboy with a reasonable grasp of computers could probably crack.

He thought he would try looking at it later on.

'Do you want me to make some calls to let people know about Helen's passing?' O'Brian said.

'That would be great.'

The priest left the room with the phone and the address book, heading back to the bedroom.

'I can't believe she's gone,' Maggie said. 'She was getting on in years, yes, but you wouldn't think it to look at her. She was as sharp as a pin, Mike. Then that cruel disease took her.'

'Have you met her brother and sister?' Holland asked.

'No.'

'Lucky you.' He looked at the woman sitting opposite him. 'Helen thought I was keeping the girls back from visiting her, but nothing could be further from the truth. Julie's a nurse and –'

'Julie's the oldest one, isn't she?' she said, interrupting him.

'Aye. Julie's twenty-seven. Jane's twenty-four.'

Maggie smiled. 'Both names start with the same letter. Do you and your wife ever get them mixed up?'

'All the time. It drives them daft.'

'What does Jane do?'

'She's a software engineer.'

'That's the thing to do nowadays. Both of them will always be in demand.'

Holland nodded.

Maggie leaned in a bit closer. 'I have to tell you something.'

'Go ahead.'

'Your mother didn't trust her brother. She thought he might come up here and start raking about in the house. And she was right. So she bought an old laptop off a friend and left it lying around.'

'Like a decoy?'

'Exactly. She hoped if he did come in here and he found that old laptop, he wouldn't look for another one. I think it worked. He has the old one with nothing much on it. You have her real one.'

Holland nodded. 'I just need to figure out how to get into it.'

O'Brian came back in. 'That's some calls made. I put a little tick by the names I could get hold of.'

'Thanks, Dan.'

'Maybe we should get hold of the funeral direc-tor. The hospital will have your mother in their mortuary, but they'll be expecting her to be taken away by the funeral director.'

Holland looked at O'Brian and Maggie in turn. 'Anybody know a good one?'

'I'll call for you, Mike. Here, check your mother's car out.' O'Brian tossed Holland the car keys. 'She kept them hanging on a hook in the kitchen.'

Holland caught the keys and stood up. 'Thanks, Dan. I appreciate it.'

'They're in the High Street,' Maggie said. 'The funeral director's. Helen expressed an interest in using that one.'

Holland left the house and opened the Vauxhall, looking at the Baxters' house to see if they were spying, but there was no sign of them. Maybe old man Baxter had taken his chainsaw to his wife.

Holland got in behind the wheel and ratcheted

the seat back. The car smelled of perfume, the same stuff his mother had worn. He gripped the wheel, holding it like she would have. He felt grief strike him inside, knowing that he was sitting where his mother had sat, then it passed.

His mother had hidden the laptop she didn't want her brother to see. What if she had hidden something else? Years ago, when they had been talking about his biological father, she had told him she would write it all down for him. Write a journal where she would explain everything.

He had never seen a journal. Had she just been full of wind? Or had she written it and kept it away from prying eyes?

He reached over and opened the glovebox. Nothing in it but papers and some napkins from McDonald's.

If he was going to hide something in a car, where would he hide it?

He got back out, the drizzle trying to envelop him, and opened the hatchback. There was litter in the back, plastic bags and a pair of dirty welly boots. Some old wrappers.

He lifted the carpet and looked into the wheel well, where the spare wheel was. And there it was: a book shape wrapped in a carrier bag. He picked it up and let the carpet go. He took the book out and saw it was the journal his mother had promised she would write.

He opened the first page and read the first few words: *Hello, Mike. Here it is, the truth. You wanted to know everything there is to know about your father. Well, here goes. Something that you should know above all else. Your father was a detective, and a good one at that.*

He was also a serial killer.

SEVEN

DCI Jimmy Dunbar and his team were a few miles south of New Lanark, their cars parked at a lodge. The old couple who owned the lodge thought it was very exciting to have the police park their cars outside in the parking area. Nothing much ever happened round here, they said, and the woman of the house scuttled around, making tea for the officers who were stationed in their living room and getting ready to make tea for the other two at a moment's notice.

The log fire was roaring away in the living room, the logs spitting and hissing like they wanted to sneak down from the grate that was holding them at bay and burn the house down.

Dunbar sat on one of the padded dining chairs,

telling DCI Angie Fisher that since his arse was older, he should be the one who got it coddled by the padding. To which Angie smiled and whispered when the two old folks weren't listening, 'I haven't heard such pish since I was in the training college.'

Dunbar just grinned and took a Hobnob with his coffee and put his headphones back on. Angie shook her head and put hers back on. They both stared at the computer screen.

'I wish his hands were a bit steadier,' Dunbar said out loud into the attached microphone.

Angie looked at him. 'He can hear you. It's set up that way.'

'Aye, I forgot. O'Connor, keep your –' He looked around to see they weren't being watched by the owners again. '...fucking hand steady. It's like you've had a stroke up there.'

'He probably has had a few strokes up there.' The voice of DS Robbie Evans came through loud and clear.

'Here, that's enough of that in front of senior officers,' Dunbar chided. He shook his head and took the headphones off.

'This is a waste of bloody time,' he said.

Angie took hers off. 'What's wrong, Jimmy?'

'We've been here for three days, and nobody's turned up with any shipment.'

'It's a pain in the arse right enough. Davie Ross isn't happy about it. Wasting man hours, and wasting *our* time. They could have had some grunts doing all this.'

Dunbar looked at his watch. 'Another two hours and we're calling it a day.'

'Agreed.'

The wind shook the tree, and by association shook DC Hamish O'Connor.

'Sarge?' he called down to Evans.

'What is it now?' Evans said, trying to be as inconspicuous as possible with his combat gear on. Hamish had his on too, but his shock of ginger hair stood out like Basil Brush in a henhouse.

'I need a pish.'

'What? Oh, for God's sake, you just got up there, Hame.'

'It's all that bloody tea the old woman gave us. Tea goes right through me.'

'Why didn't you go to the lavvy before you got up there?'

'I did. Now I need it again. I think it's the cold that's making me need it.'

'Mother of Christ.' Evans heard the noise of the engine again. He assumed O'Connor had heard it too, but there was no sign of the younger detective pulling his woollen hat on.

'Hame! The tractor's coming round again.'

The tractor was just for show, Evans knew. The old farm had gone under months ago, and the gorilla driving it would be more at home standing at the door of a nightclub than working on farm machinery, but they were keeping up the pretence of a working farm, in case anybody guessed correctly the place was being used for a money-laundering operation.

'Oh God. I don't know if I can hold it in or not.'

'You better not pish on me.' Evans stood back just in case. He hid behind the thick tree as the tractor drove by, then turned and headed up over the hill.

'Stand back, Robbie, I'm going to have to let fly.'

'Jam the camera between two branches or something. And use the bloody hand sanitiser you always carry.'

'Oh, Mummy, Daddy, I can't get it out fast enough. Christ, I think my zip's jammed.'

'Hurry up, fuck. But wait until I get further away.'

'That's a mixed signal: hurry up but wait.'

'Right, I'm moving, and I better not be downwind of your pish storm.'

'Christ, Robbie, I think I've ripped my trousers. The bastard zip's come away.'

'Never mind, they're old army trousers. I'm going to incinerate these later. Yours have already been designated medical waste. Now fucking hurry up. Wait until I tell you I'm far enough away.'

There were bushes round the base of the trees providing plenty of hiding spaces from Tractor Man and anybody who would be looking through binoculars in the farmhouse in the distance. The road was a one-lane affair with very little traffic flow.

'Right, get a move on,' Evans said, then spotted Angie Fisher walking towards them at a fair clip.

'Christ, shotie, shotie!' Evans said in an urgent voice before Angie got within earshot.

'What is it?' Hamish said.

Evans ignored the question, knowing the DCI would hear him now.

Both Evans and Angie heard the crack of the branch and the scream. They looked up to see

Hamish hanging on to a branch for dear life, his underpants and trousers round his ankles.

'As an entrance, that's a belter, Hamish,' Angie said. The DC's face was the same colour as his hair now.

'Help!' he squealed, trying not to shout but to convey urgently that he was in dire straits. Neither of his colleagues was in any doubt that the younger DC had fucked up.

Angie grinned. 'Better get up there and help him, Robbie.'

Evans looked up again and saw that the branch Hamish had been standing on was on the ground and the DC was holding on to the other branch like his life depended on it.

'Please don't take any photos, ma'am,' Evans said as he fought through the bushes and started climbing the tree.

'I don't want to be responsible for putting photos of that wee thing on the internet.'

'I heard that,' Hamish said.

When he had reached the sturdy branch that Hamish had started out along, Evans carefully clung on and inched his way along.

'Start swinging,' Evans instructed. 'Your legs, I mean. Nothing else.'

'It's hard when my legs are stuck together at the ankles.'

'Try, Hamish,' Angie said. 'Before the polis come along and arrest you for indecent exposure.' She grinned up at him.

Hamish lifted his knees and let his legs fall back, trying to get some momentum going, and give the boy a coconut, he actually managed to get a little bit of a swing going before that branch broke off too.

Hamish screamed all the way to the ground, which wasn't that far, and his fall was broken by bushes. He landed with a dull thud as the bushes were crushed underneath him and he narrowly avoided having his willy chopped off.

He lay groaning as Evans made his way back down the tree, careful not to suffer the same fate as his colleague, but he had no intention of either unzipping his trousers or pulling his pants down in public.

On firm ground again, he looked over at Angie.

'Go and help your friend, Robbie,' she said, smiling.

'Och, in the name o' the wee man.' Evans shook his head. 'Hamish, please tell me you've managed to pull your skids up.'

'I'm dying here, Robbie,' Hamish answered in a strained voice. 'Go, save yourself.'

'You're fucking delirious, man.'

'I think I landed in a bunch of jaggie nettles. My baws are stinging, and I think my bellend snapped off. Help me, Robbie. I'm feared to move.'

'In case the nettles move and sting you up the arse as well?'

'That ship already sailed. I think I've lost all feeling in my legs. Ma'am, could you call for an ambulance? I don't think I'll ever be able to walk again. If I even survive. Somebody please tell me they'll look after my wee dug –'

Evans reached down and grabbed one of Hamish's arms and yanked him upright.

'If anybody asks, your fucking Ys were already up by the time I got to you,' Evans said in a low voice which was almost a feral growl.

'Can you see any docken leaves? They're supposed to ease the pain. My bollocks are stinging. Help me get my pants up, Robbie.'

'Did you not just hear what I fucking said? Pull them up yourself.' Evans navigated through the brush, leaving his colleague to get himself together.

A few minutes later, Hamish came traipsing out at a much slower pace than Evans had. 'I couldn't find any docken leaves. And I might have broke my coccyx.'

Evans turned to look at him. 'I thought you were going to say you broke your –'

'Robbie,' Angie said, cutting in.

Both men looked at her.

'They're sending a team here to replace us. We got a shout. Before we go to the scene, you might want to get changed. Oh, and Hamish? Try Sudocrem. I hear it works wonders for nettle rash.'

'Promise me you'll give me a good send-off,' Hamish said, but it fell on deaf ears.

EIGHT

DCI Mike Holland took a deep breath as he stood at the entrance door to the funeral parlour. He looked at Dan O'Brian. 'I appreciate you coming with me.'

'It's not a problem, Mike.'

'Normally, as part of my duties, I would be able to walk into one of these places no problem. It's just that, you know, with it being Helen –'

The priest clapped a hand on Holland's shoulder. 'I understand. Now, come on, let's not keep the man waiting.'

It was like a small industrial unit, some place you might think sold double glazing or was a plumber's office had it not been for the funeral director's sign outside.

They went into the front office, and it was warm

out of the biting cold. An older woman sat behind a desk and smiled at them as they came in.

'Good morning, Father. Good morning, sir.'

'Good morning,' O'Brian said, taking the lead. In a way, they both had a job that required them to take the lead, one of them sending people to prison, the other sending them to meet their maker. Holland was a step back from the priest and felt comfortable relinquishing power to his new friend. It meant he didn't have to think too hard about what was to happen next.

'DCI Holland called earlier about having his mother picked up from the hospital and he's come in to make funeral arrangements.'

'Oh, yes. I'm so sorry for your loss. But I'll let Mr Drummond come and speak with you.' She lifted the receiver while the two men looked at posters on the wall advertising different funeral services.

'He'll be right with you,' the woman said, replacing the receiver.

'Thank you,' Holland said. He looked at a poster for coffins and felt his stomach churn. His mother would soon be in a box like that, before she was pushed into the fire that would consume her and turn her into ashes.

The door to the back opened and a tall, skinny

man wearing a black suit appeared. He gave a smile as he approached, his hand out. 'Mr Holland?'

He held his hand towards Holland, correctly guessing that the man with the dog collar was there in a support capacity.

Holland shook it. 'Thank you for seeing me.'

'Oh, no problem. We're here to make your life a little bit easier in such a troubled time.'

Holland wondered how many times the man had said that in his career, and whether he said it on autopilot now.

Drummond let go of Holland's hand and gestured for them to follow him through to the back. Holland led the way, O'Brian bringing up the rear.

The office could have been a bank, or a manager's office in a nondescript office block. There were two fake-leather chairs sitting opposite Drummond's.

They sat down and a slight smell hit Holland's nostrils. Some chemical smell. Embalming fluid maybe.

'Mr Holland, let me start by saying that we picked your mum up from the hospital after your phone call and she's with us now. We just have to go over some finer details before we proceed.'

Holland looked blankly at Drummond for a

moment, until he remembered what he'd had to do with his adoptive parents. 'The coffin?'

'Yes. I have a book with different designs in it –'

Holland held up a hand, stopping the man in his tracks. 'It was my mother's wishes that she be cremated. She wouldn't have wanted an expensive coffin used for her.'

'Absolutely. We have a range of coffins that are still perfect for a decent send-off but won't break the bank.'

Drummond brought the book out and showed Holland some coffins and he chose one. When he had been going through her personal papers, he had found a will, and an insurance policy. The money would be more than enough to cover her funeral expenses.

'I also mentioned repatriation,' Holland said.

'Yes, we can do that. Where would you like your mother to go?'

'Dunfermline, where she came from.'

'We can do that. We can arrange the funeral, have her transported down, everything. All you need to do is leave everything with us. We'll sort everything. Can I ask when you yourself will be going down to Dunfermline?'

'Probably in the next couple of days. I live in

Glasgow, so I'll be going home first. Then I'll come up for the funeral.'

'Very well.'

Holland looked at O'Brian. 'Would you do the service?'

The priest smiled. 'It would be my pleasure. Father McLean will be back on Sunday. When I explained about Helen, he said he felt he was well enough to get back in the saddle, as it were.'

'Terrific. Thank you.'

With just a few forms to fill in, Holland was free to go.

Outside, the cold bit into them.

'I just have to organise getting rid of her things,' Holland said. 'Maybe a charity could come and pick them up. I'll dump whatever isn't taken.'

'There's a small company down in Tain who do estate clear-outs. I can give them a call if you like?'

'I appreciate it. Listen, why don't you let me buy you a pint tonight? I'll head down the road tomorrow.'

'Sounds good to me, my friend.'

Holland felt the thirst grab hold of him, but he just wanted a few pints, not to drive his car the next morning like it only had hand controls.

'I'd like to go back to Helen's and see if there's anything worth keeping.'

'Let's do that. Maggie Quinn should still be there, sorting piles for the charity shops,' O'Brian said.

The end of a life, getting sorted into bin bags. *No wonder I drink,* Holland thought to himself.

NINE

It was late afternoon when Harry McNeil got back to the incident room with Elvis, sure that the cold had shrivelled him in a place that wouldn't please his wife, Alex.

'While you were across the water having ice cream and going on the rides, we were busy with the whiteboard,' DI Charlie Skellett said, hobbling across the room.

'It's a bit early for the fairground on the Links, Charlie,' Harry said. He was about to ask Elvis to put the kettle on, but the young lad was already there.

Harry shook his overcoat off and walked over to where Lillian O'Shea and DS Julie Stott were standing, attaching photos with magnets.

'Aye, that one's a belter,' Skellett said. The photo

was a close-up of the entry wound, with the arrow sticking out in an almost horizontal position.

'It smelled like God alone knows what,' Frank Miller said. 'Shite mostly.'

'I would shite myself if some nutcase was pointing a crossbow at me,' Skellett said.

'Listen, everybody,' Harry said, getting everybody's attention. 'DI Miller has given you the rundown on the situation with Craig Smith, but I just wanted to reiterate what Neil McGovern told us: this information goes no further than this room. Understood?'

They all agreed that this case was eyes only and wouldn't be the topic of conversation outside.

'It would help if McGovern would give us some more info to work on,' Skellett said.

'We're treating this as another normal murder investigation,' Harry said.

'Except we don't know much about him and probably won't,' Skellett said. 'We don't know why he ended up in a manky old caravan in an old campground. Who did he piss off that badly he ended up with an arrow going through his head?'

'Maybe he owed somebody money?' Julie said.

Harry looked sceptical. 'That's usually just a tap on the kneecaps with a hammer to gently remind somebody they're behind with the rent. This was more personal.'

'Sometimes more personal means stabbing the victim fifty times,' Elvis said, pouring the coffees. 'Anybody else want one?'

The others shook their heads. They'd clearly already stopped for their break before he and Harry had arrived back.

'I've seen a few of those, right enough,' Skellett said. 'There are some mad bastards around, let me tell you. When I was in Glasgow with Calvin, we got called to a house where a husband had given his wife a belting with an axe. Twelve cuts in her with this thing. And guess what it was over?'

They all looked at him as if he had just revealed he was the hands behind Punch and Judy.

'The TV remote,' he answered. 'I kid you not. Nowadays I just let the wife have the remote. I don't fancy getting my willy chopped off with an axe or any other sharp implement.'

'She'd have to put her reading glasses on to see it first, wouldn't she?' Lillian said.

'Oh, that's funny. Let me tell you something –'

Harry put up a hand to divert their attention away from Skellett's impending appointment with his wife's carving knife or, God forbid, the knitting needle he used to scratch his leg behind the knee brace.

'Let's just focus. We seem to have gone off at a tangent here,' Harry said.

'Did you see a TV in that caravan?' Julie said. 'Maybe Craig wouldn't hand over the remote.'

'I think that's enough about remotes,' Harry said, taking a coffee from Elvis. 'Cheers, son.'

'I did some research on the assault that Smith was arrested for,' Miller said.

All eyes were on him now.

'Smith worked in an office in Fountainbridge. The woman he assaulted was a co-worker. They were working late and he said she was giving him the come-on, but she denied it. She called the police, and when they turned up, she was bleeding from a cut lip. He'd hit her and tried to strangle her, she said. He was arrested, but when he went to court, he pleaded not guilty, saying the cut lip was from them both getting rough. Ultimately, there was no proof he assaulted her, so they dropped the case.'

'Where does she live?' Harry asked.

Miller looked at him. 'She killed herself a month later. It was in the papers.'

'Does she have a husband, or family in the area?' Harry asked.

'She was engaged, according to the news article.'

'Try and find him and any other family member. One of them might hold a grudge.'

'Will do.'

Harry's phone rang and he answered it, walking away from the others when he saw it was a call from his wife. 'Hello?' he said, keeping it professional.

'Hi, honey,' Alex said, apparently not singing from the same hymn sheet.

'I'm assuming you're calling with a result from the number plate?'

'I am indeed. The number belongs to a girl called Amanda Brown.'

'Is it connected to Craig Smith's house in Burntisland?' Harry asked.

'No. She lives in Glasgow.'

TEN

'Won't they miss you through in Edinburgh?' Detective Superintendent Lynn McKenzie said.

'I've left the department in the good hands of Harry McNeil,' DSup Calvin Stewart said, pulling her closer. 'Anybody would think you're trying to get rid of me.'

She laughed. 'I wish you could stay through here again. Maybe if...'

He put a finger on her lips. 'Edinburgh to Glasgow isn't that far. I'm sure I'd be under your feet if I was through here all the time. Besides, they like you in Helen Street, and they can't stand me. Old motormouth himself.'

'I know you're right.' She kissed him and he let her go. 'It's worked so far, hasn't it?'

'It has.'

She grabbed her jacket and put it on. 'Same car?'

'Maybe better to go separately. Tongues wagging and all that.'

'The only tongue that's wagging is Davie Ross's, and that's only about his retirement. And we don't want to be late to his party this afternoon.'

'I'm going to miss the old sod. I've heard his replacement is a real tough one.'

'She might just be tough with you.' She smiled, still finding it hard to believe that she was going to be the new detective chief superintendent, not just the acting one, covering for Davie Ross while he had been recuperating after getting stabbed last Christmas. Three months later and he was fit enough to head off into retirement.

They headed out of Lynn's house into the chilly Glasgow afternoon. Lunch had been soup and a sandwich, and no benefits, much to Stewart's disappointment.

'You deserve the promotion, Lynn, but don't let it go to your head in the bedroom.'

'Don't worry, I'll still give you nine out of ten.'

'Nine?' Stewart said with mock indignation.

'There's always room for improvement.'

'Deary me. I think somebody's needing put

across my knee.'

She laughed as they got into their cars, and they drove off through the afternoon traffic, which was well on its way to getting upgraded from 'pain in the arse' to 'Do you want me to teach you how to fucking drive?'.

The incident room at Helen Street was quieter than normal, with DI Lisa McDonald holding the fort.

'Have they checked in from the stakeout yet?' Stewart asked.

'No, sir. I don't think much is going on. From what DCI Dunbar told me earlier, Robbie and Hamish are taking turns in climbing a tree with the cameras.'

'Aw, Jesus. I hope that pair know what they're doing. Knowing them, they would have put two animals of the same sex on the ark.'

'Fingers crossed they get some photos or videos.'

'Right then, let's get upstairs. Lynn McKenzie is already away up and Davie Ross's last few minutes of being a copper are counting down to zero. I hope he hasn't chugged all the fucking champagne. Come on, Lisa, let's go and get a glass.'

'Maybe a Coke for me.'

'That just means more for us.' He chuckled. 'Getting pished on duty in front of the boss. Result.'

Upstairs, a conference room had been set up with a buffet, now half-eaten as various bodies had come in, shaken Ross's hand and grabbed some scran on the way out.

Stewart and Lisa got in just ahead of Lynn. There were some civilian staff standing around, a low hum of conversation reverberating around the room.

Ross's girlfriend, Joan Devine, had already retired from the fiscal's office and they were making plans to go and catch some sun somewhere.

'Hi, Joan.'

'Hi, Calvin. How have you been?'

'Not too shabby. Yourself?'

'Oh, you know; making sure this one takes his painkillers.' She smiled at Ross.

'Och, away, woman. You would think I'm a bairn the way she acts,' Ross complained.

'It's not every day you get stabbed. You need somebody to keep on top of the medications.'

'I'm a hundred per cent better now. But time to hand over the reins. And talking of which...here she is.'

Ross picked up a glass and tapped it with a spoon. 'Ladies and gentlemen, as you all know, this is my last day with Police Scotland and my position of detective chief superintendent goes to Lynn McKenzie. She performed brilliantly in the exams and passed with flying colours. So please, can we all welcome my replacement, the newest DCS in Helen Street, Lynn McKenzie.'

They all clapped, and Stewart thought back to the nights he had spent in Lynn's house, and in his own flat in Edinburgh, going over scenarios they might throw at her during the interview section. There had been times when she thought she was going to break down, but Stewart had been there for her, bolstering her. He'd taken on the role of some nasty bastard assistant chief as he tried to break her down, to make her cry, but she had been strong, and after a few blips, she had carried on. In the real interview, they hadn't given her as hard a time as Stewart had, so she sailed through it.

She smiled at him as she stepped to the front of the room. 'Thank you all for being here today. I know my other colleagues will be joining in on the celebrations later, but they're on assignment today so they couldn't be here. But to all of you who are here now, thank you for your support in the past few months as

I studied for the promotion board. It was tough going, but I had my rock to help me through it.'

'Oh, don't mention it,' Ross said, and Joan nudged him in the ribs.

'Well, I was *one* of her rocks,' he whispered.

'You were a mere flatty that skipped over the water before sinking.' Joan grinned at him.

'If I wasn't retiring, you'd be under arrest right now for treason.'

'I think you'll make a fantastic DCS,' Stewart said. 'Can I suggest a toast?'

'Yes!' Ross said. 'We have non-alcoholic grape juice and Pepsi. The glasses have been filled, so grab what you fancy.' He looked at Joan. 'I mean drink wise, young lady.'

'Away with yourself. Keep your strength for later.'

'I put a bottle of champagne in the fridge,' Stewart complained to Lisa.

'And we'll enjoy it later on, thanks very much,' Ross said.

'Oh bollocks. Your round in the pub later on, Davie-boy,' Stewart said, grabbing a glass of what he thought of as cat pish.

'To Lynn!' Ross shouted.

'To Lynn!' they all shouted.

Then Stewart's phone rang. Angie Fisher. 'I was going to say, you're missing all the fun, but not really.' He screwed his face up at the glass of what could only be described as recycled pish water.

'No alcohol?' Angie said.

'Correct.'

'The pub has alcohol, and trust me, there's a pint with my name on it.'

'What, nothing delicate for you? Like a wee gin?'

'Why would you think that of me? Do I look like a woman who drinks gin?'

'No' really, no. You calling with an update on that farmhouse?'

'Yes and no.'

'No riddles now, Chief Inspector.'

'We got a request from Harry McNeil's wife in Fife. She asked if one of our CID gang could go and talk with a female who apparently was connected with a death they're investigating. When CID got there, her door was open and they found her inside. Very much dead.'

'Murder?' Stewart asked.

'She has a crossbow arrow through her head. Just like the Edinburgh victim.'

'Text me the address. I'll be right over.'

ELEVEN

Mike Holland stood in the living room of his mother's house. It all seemed so final now.

'I really appreciate this,' Holland said to O'Brian and Maggie Quinn.

'My flock can be counted when others need help,' O'Brian said with a smile. He looked at Maggie. 'Are you all going to miss me when I go back to Fife?'

'Of course we are,' Maggie said. 'Father McLean is a lot more traditional. It was a nice wee change to have you here.'

'I have to admit, I was quite happy to stand in, and it has been a pleasure meeting you all, but now Father McLean is well again, time for me to go home.'

'Helen would have missed you so much,' Maggie said. 'She spoke very highly of you.'

'I appreciate that.' O'Brian looked at Holland. 'You hear that, Mike? Your mother spoke highly of me. That means a lot.'

'I'm sure she was very pleased to have you up here, Father,' Holland answered.

He looked at Maggie. 'Can any of you use my mother's car? I don't want anything for it.'

Maggie looked at O'Brian, who in turn looked at Holland. 'Didn't Maggie say? She said you had mentioned getting rid of it, and I thought you meant you'd sell it, so I took the liberty of making a bid. I wrote it down and put it in an envelope. It's beside the telephone. I hope you don't mind.'

Holland crossed to the phone, picked up the envelope, took out the piece of paper and read the figure that was written on it. He looked at the priest. 'This is too much. It's not worth anywhere near that, I'm sure.' He was kicking himself for not looking up the price, thinking it was an old scrapper, but apparently not.

'Look, I've been having engine trouble on my car for a little while now. Isn't that right, Maggie?'

The woman nodded. 'Indeed. Clapped out, just like me.'

O'Brian laughed. 'If the sum is acceptable, I'd like to take the car off your hands, Mike.'

'That's very generous, thank you.' They shook on it and Holland gave him the car keys.

'I'm sure this will be a lot more reliable transport to get me back to Glenrothes than the death trap I was driving. It got me here on a wing and a prayer. Mostly prayer.'

'Help yourself to anything else you might want.' Holland looked at Maggie. 'You said the charity shop van is coming for the stuff tomorrow?'

'They are.'

'Thank you for all your help.'

'Anytime,' Maggie said, and then she started sorting the clothes into different piles.

O'Brian came across to Holland, who was staring out of the living room window. 'It's a sad time, Mike, and you know you can call me anytime, even when we're down the road. Glasgow isn't that far from Glenrothes. I promise I won't desert you after the funeral.'

Holland faced him. 'Thank you. I appreciate that. But I have my uncle Dick on my mind.'

'He does seem to be the sort of person you would want to steer clear of.'

'It's not that, Dan. The last time I came up here, Helen told me she had been putting money away for a day exactly like this. She had a little bit of life insurance, but she also had money left over from when she sold her house. It was a few grand. I told her she would be better keeping it in the bank, but she insisted on keeping it in a money box. Now there's no sign of it. She kept it in her wardrobe, and I don't see any reason for her to have moved it, but now it's gone. I think Dick took it.'

O'Brian took a deep breath and blew it out. 'That would be low, Mike. If your uncle took it then that's theft, plain and simple. But how can you prove it?'

'I can't, that's the thing.'

'It's shocking what some people will stoop to. He's going to have to answer the man when he gets upstairs, Mike.'

'To be honest, I don't know why he didn't just take her car.'

'Me too. But if he had a car, he couldn't drive two back.'

'That's the thing: the last I heard, he didn't have a car. Helen told me that Dick was always complaining he couldn't afford a new car, even a second-hand one.'

'He could hide the cash, but he couldn't exactly hide the car,' O'Brian said. 'How did he get up here?'

'Train. He always came up by train. Then my mother would drive him around.'

'I've met people like him before, Mike,' O'Brian said. 'He'll be going straight down to hell.'

Holland nodded. 'I'm going to the guesthouse. See you for dinner later?'

'Count on it.'

Holland thanked O'Brian and Maggie again and headed out, feeling the need for some fresh air.

He jumped into his car, giving his mother's car another look. The Vauxhall was in pretty good shape and he was pleased O'Brian wanted it, and if he was going to give Holland some money for it then fine, and it was going to a good home. It could have gone to some young yahoo who would have put on an exhaust that made the ears bleed and wheels that cost more than Holland's monthly pay.

He drove the five minutes to the guesthouse. There was nobody around, so he quietly made his way up to the room, where he switched on the little travel kettle and put a sachet of coffee into a mug.

He felt like getting wired into a few nips, but fought the urge. He wanted to be sober when he called his uncle. He sat on the bed, not making eye contact with the wallpaper, and took his shoes off before hitting the contact button for Dick.

'*Hello?*' The voice was gruff, cut with alcohol. It seemed that his uncle couldn't care less who he was going to talk to and had administered himself a few whiskies, despite it being late afternoon.

'It's me, Mike.'

Dick made a grunting noise, like he had just stepped onto chewing gum and no matter how much he pulled at the stringy rubber, the bastard stuff still wouldn't come off.

'*I know it's you. I saw your fucking name. What do you want?*'

'I arranged my mother's funeral. She'll be getting cremated in Dunfermline. I'll call you when the date is confirmed. It won't be long. Call your sister. Let her know.'

'*You better be giving her a good send-off.*'

Holland felt the anger rising. 'Did you steal the money box my mother had hidden in her wardrobe?'

'*You little bastard.*'

'Well, somebody fucking took it and we all know you're the tea leaf in the family. And I'd like to see you fucking try.'

'*I'll have my niece's husband kick your head in.*'

There were a million retorts flying through

Holland's mind, some witty, some raging, but none of them complimentary, so he just hung up. The last one on his mind was, 'I'll take your baws off with a fucking chainsaw', but that would mean asking old man Baxter next door if he could borrow *his* chainsaw. The logistics of taking it down to Dunfermline and getting back up north never entered the equation.

He made his coffee and found the diary/journal in his case. He took it out, put his coffee on the bedside cabinet and sat on the bed with his feet up. Was this account of his father true, or yet another attempt at destroying the mental image he'd built up of the old man? He'd never seen a photo of him. Nobody seemed to have heard of DCI Phil Nichol. But his father had retired a long time ago, enjoying a few years of retirement before dying.

If Holland hadn't listened to his mother, he could have met the old man, but he had listened to her protestations and had stayed away.

Now he was reading the words his mother had written. They'd had a chat one night on the phone, and she had said, maybe I'll write it down and you'll understand what a real bastard he was. But you can only read it when I'm gone. I won't have a conversation about it.

Now here he was, reading it.

Your father was a serial killer.

The thought angered Holland as he took a sip of the coffee. Helen had hated Phil, but not enough to stop seeing him after Holland was born. *Oh no, Helen, you kept going back for more, didn't you?*

Every time she had spoken of Phil Nichol, there had been poison dripping from her words, but how could she have hated the man so much when she had continued seeing him?

And had a second son by him?

Holland had been genuinely excited when his mother said he had a brother. But the boy had died at only a few months old. Almost five years after Holland had been born. If Phil Nichol had been so bad, why had Helen entertained the idea of going with him again and bearing him another child? It didn't make sense at first, but then it had become crystal clear: she had been in love with him, but the feelings hadn't been reciprocated. Helen had stuck it out for a long time, waiting for Nichol, waiting for a day when he would tell her that she was the one and they would run away together. But that day never came. So she had poisoned Holland against his own father.

And he had fallen for it.

Nichol had two sons, and they were older than Holland. *They won't want to meet you,* Helen had said. *You'll cause a lot of trouble.*

His ancestry DNA kit had put him in touch with his younger half-brother. The man – Hugh Nichol – had told him that they didn't have a brother and this must be a mistake. But their older brother, Walter Nichol, had told Hugh that yes, they did indeed have a brother.

So began a journey of sending and receiving emails over the past few months, getting to know each other, building up to meeting in person. That day had come and Holland had met Walter and Hugh in the Kirkcaldy Galleries.

Holland was excited about meeting his extended family, at least on one side. He'd had an adopted sister, but she had turned into a junkie and had died of an overdose years ago, so he had no other siblings.

He opened the book and started reading, knowing he should read this with a pinch of salt as it had been written by a bitter old woman. It was written ten years ago, many years after Phil Nichol had died, but still, Helen couldn't let go of the fact that she had been dumped for another woman, a woman who was actually married to Nichol. And that had been her downfall.

TWELVE

DSup Calvin Stewart normally worked out of Edinburgh. He'd worked in Glasgow Division all his working life but had taken a transfer through to the Edinburgh Division. If it hadn't been for seeing off Davie Ross, he wouldn't have been here today.

He got out of his car into a biting wind, the icy cold scurrying round the tight, narrow streets of the council scheme. It was hard to get parked for the cars parking on the pavement, so he'd pulled through in front of a police van and parked in the middle of the road.

'Get either end of this place blocked off,' he told a uniform. 'I don't want to come out and find this fucking thing up on bricks.'

'Yes, sir,' the young guy said.

Stewart walked towards the communal stairway where another uniform was standing guard. He nodded towards Stewart. 'First floor, sir,' he said.

'Aye. It can never be on the fucking ground floor. Make an old bastard like me climb the stairs.'

He trudged in, his shoes scuffing the stone steps as he made his way up through the smell. It was like somebody was making cabbage soup or some such shite. Whatever it was, it was honking the whole stair out.

He got to the landing where the activity was. Uniforms, scene of crime in their white suits, and his team somewhere in the middle of the scrum.

He still thought of them as 'his team' even though they hadn't been his team for a long time. At the end of the day, Calvin Stewart did what he wanted to do, and most people just put their fingers in their ears and hoped the fallout didn't affect them.

Angie Fisher met him in the hallway. 'It's a bad one, sir.'

'You told me the lassie has an arrow in her heid.'

'She does. She was shot at relatively close range. It took part of her skull off at the exit point.'

'Jesus. Where are the others?'

'Jimmy Dunbar is organising a door-to-door and they're with him and uniforms.'

'Got a name for her?'

'Amanda Brown.'

'Right, let's have a look.'

The flat was council-chic, with wallpaper that might have been fashionable in the 80s and carpet that no self-respecting dog would drag its arse over. The smell was of stale cigarette smoke, alcohol and a distinct odour of death.

Dr Fiona Christie was one of the city pathologists. She was standing looking at the victim when Stewart approached.

'Hey, Calvin. I've not seen you around here for a while. I thought you were in Edinburgh now?'

'Hi, Fiona. Yes, I am, but I was through here seeing Davie Ross off. He's been keeping his seat warm for Lynn McKenzie. She's taking over from him.'

'That's terrific. Now she's your boss. I think we all know who'll be doing the dishes in your house from now on.' She smiled at him.

'Come on now, let's not get carried away. Besides, she lives here and I live in Edinburgh.'

'You can't live that way forever, though. Long-distance relationships only last for so long.'

'And you would know this why?'

'I look at the internet. It's full of stuff like this.' She grinned.

'Aye, aye. Just tell us about this lassie here.'

Fiona's grin disappeared. 'This is a strange one, Calvin. Very unusual form of murder, I have to say. The closest thing I've seen to this was when a young man was accidentally shot through the eye with an arrow. That was on a hunting trip. This was no accident. This was done in a rage, I would say. She looks to have been shot at close range. If you look at her left hand, you can see where the arrow went right through, as if she had been holding her hand up to ward off her attacker. It went right through and into her skull, coming out the back. Instant death.' She looked at him. 'Have you ever seen a death like this?'

Stewart had been given a heads-up on the caravan death by Harry McNeil and told about Neil McGovern's involvement. 'No. This is a first.' He shook his head. 'She looks like she's been dead for a while.'

'Correct. I'd say a couple of weeks at least.'

Stewart looked at the female. Her skin was a pale grey and she looked bloated, as if the gases were starting to expand in her. He couldn't tell for sure, of course, but he knew the longer a corpse lay undisturbed, the greater the chance of the gases expanding, causing an explosion.

Stewart's phone rang. He excused himself and took the call out in the hall. 'Hello?'

'*Calvin, it's Neil McGovern.*'

'Neil. Good to hear from you again. What's up?'

'*You're at the house of a young girl, correct? Amanda Brown?*'

'I am indeed. And now you're calling me asking about her, meaning she's somehow connected to you.'

'*Spot on, old son. There was a victim outside Edinburgh, a young man with an arrow in his head. They're connected. We need to do a secure Zoom meeting, you, me and Harry McNeil.*'

'I can have Angie Fisher and Jimmy Dunbar run this end of things.'

'*Good. I've also had a news blackout put in place, just like for the Edinburgh one. Keep the team tight, and tell those uniformed monkeys that if word gets out, I will find out who did it, and their career will be finished and they'll be spending some time in the Bar-L. I can't stress that enough.*'

'I'll spread the word, Neil.'

'*Good. Get back to Helen Street. I know you were only there for Davie Ross retiring, but I want you to run things at that end. Liaise with Harry. I'm at*

Fettes Station now, so we'll wait for you to call us when you get back.'

'I'm on my way.'

He hung up and told Angie about her and Dunbar wrapping things up here.

'You wouldn't be sneaking off to have a fly one with Lynn now, would you?'

'Depends what you mean by fly one. Cup of tea? Chocolate Hobnob?'

'I know it's not that, because all we have left are Rich Tea and the team would rather eat a gangrened foot than eat that cardboard.'

'Right, keep it above gutter level. And even if I was, you wouldn't be the one I'd tell.'

'Glad you trust me, boss.'

'As much as I could spit you.' He grinned at her as he walked out of the house. What the hell was going on with the two victims being murdered in the same way? A serial killer starting out, or had he killed more in the same way and they just hadn't found out yet?

He got back in his car and drove back to the station.

THIRTEEN

Mike Holland took another sip of his whisky. He'd read the opening paragraph six times, not sure if he should carry on or not. His mother had tried to taint the image of his father from the first day he had met her, almost thirty-three years ago. He had told her back in the early days that he was going to see him whether she liked it or not, but then she had hit the bottle and had begged him not to do it. He had relented, and then his father had died and the chance had passed. Now he thought he was going to read more about how big of a bastard his father had been. And now Helen had left him a note saying Nichol had been a serial killer.

He felt a spasm of anger at her. Took another sip of whisky and started to read in earnest.

———

Well, Mike, you know the old saying, be careful what you wish for. You asked me many times if I would write your story down, so one night, after I'd had a few gins of course, I started doing just that. And this is the result. I'm going to tell you a few home truths, so brace yourself. You might not like what I have to tell you, but I can't rewrite history. You are part of my history and there's no going back and changing things. We're stuck with what hand we were dealt in life. Oh yes, you can think back and wish you could change things, but you can't. I thought the same way when I was younger, but I've had to make peace with my life.

This is the last chance you get to close the book and never open it again. If you read on from this point, then never let it be said you couldn't turn back. Because you can. Close the book, walk away and keep the memories you have untarnished. I'm telling you this right now, Mikey-boy: you can't un-ring a bell. So put the book down, burn it if you want, or read on. I made sure I started on a new page. You'll have to turn it to start reading.

Good luck with whatever decision you make.

Right, so you decided to bash on. What a brave

wee soldier you are. Where to start? At the beginning, I think.

I was nineteen when I joined the polis. Nineteen sixty. The start of the swinging sixties, and by God did we have a good time. Parties, going to the dancing, having a good laugh. I made some good friends at training and kept in touch. Four of us went to work in Dunfermline, all gung-ho, ready to change the world. Or Fife at least.

I first met Phil Nichol in the canteen one day. I literally bumped into him. I blushed and apologised, thanking God I hadn't spilled a cup of coffee down him. But it was no harm, no foul, and he just smiled and said it wasn't a problem. He was a real looker was your father. I saw him around quite a few times after that, and I was lucky enough to be sent to a crime scene and who was in charge? Yep. Phil and I got talking and he asked me what I did for fun. I told him I drank and danced and sometimes the two were a lethal combination.

It was after that I saw him at the dancing one night. I knew he was quite a bit older than me, but he was so much fun. He walked me home that night, but I had to stop round the corner from my house. I didn't want your granny and grandad to find out some older *bloke had walked me home, in case they got the wrong impression.*

And they would have been right.

Phil kissed me, and I could have pulled away then, maybe walked round the corner to my house and that would have been the end of it, but I didn't. That was a real fork-in-the-road moment.

I chose the path more travelled, as it would turn out.

I saw Phil more and more, then we started having an affair. I knew he was married. Of course I found out that he had just turned forty, so he was double my age. People say that age is just a number, and that was so true. Phil could move like a man half his age. He was tender in his love-making. You're screwing your face up just now, aren't you? Ha-ha. Keep on reading, Mike. The tale gets more sordid as we go along.

I first saw another side to Phil when we were both working one day. I was on patrol, and my partner was walking slightly ahead of me. He either didn't see what was going on or chose to ignore it. But I saw it. There was a little alleyway down between a couple of shops and Phil was kicking a man who was on the ground. He was shouting and swearing, threatening the man.

It shocked me, and I was about to shout out to

him, but I walked away. I knew then that I had peeked behind the curtain of DI Phil Nichol. Yes, he was a DI at the time. Promotion would come later, and at that time he was an inspector.

I avoided him after that, and he left messages for me, but I didn't contact him. I was scared, truth be told. Later on, when I suspected him of being a serial killer, I thought about that man in the alleyway and how lucky he was to have escaped from Phil's clutches. Others wouldn't be so lucky, but as it turned out, he chose women to kill, not men.

But I digress. I'm getting ahead of myself here. Yes, let's get back on track. Your father pursued me, and he finally caught up to me one day after I'd been avoiding him. He asked me what was wrong. I told him that I thought my dad had found out about us. He'd been acting antsy recently, and I was scared.

Big bad Phil said he would take care of me. Protect me! And get this: your grandfather was the same age as Phil. I was going out with a man who was literally old enough to be my father. But I didn't care. My father looked older because he worked down the mine. Phil looked after himself, dressed nicely and liked to splash a bit cash. It wasn't long before I was going out with him again.

And then I slept with him. In the back of his car

of all places. But it was good. I felt like a real woman, going out with a real man.

The thing is, I had tried talking to him about his wife and kids, but he said he wouldn't talk about them. I felt angry at first, but I couldn't stay mad at him. He was such a charmer was your father. I went along with it, only occasionally mentioning his kids.

This affair went on for such a long time, I was sure we were going to get caught, that his wife would come to the station and have a fight with me. But it never did happen.

The affair was heating up. But work was starting to bog him down. A girl had been found in Pittencrieff Park, what we called the Glen. You know, the park in the middle of Dunfermline. This is something you can look up. She was a young girl who had been out on the town with her friends. My partner and I were first on the scene after an anonymous phone call was made and I saw her lying in the bushes. She looked like she was a very pretty girl in life, nicely dressed. She looked like she could just have been lying down, asleep or drunk, if it hadn't been for the blooms of red on her white top.

She was staring at me, that I remember. And those beautiful earrings she wore. They were opal, set in gold. They didn't look cheap, like a street walker might wear. This girl was no whore.

I radioed it in, calling for CID, and then guess who turned up? The man himself. I have to admit, my heart missed a beat seeing him. If I had known then what I knew later, I would have run away from him as fast as possible.

After he turned up with his DS, they called in forensics and a pathologist. It got late and dark, but they had lights, and the pathologist – an old man called Dean – clucked about like a hen. Then he cleared her for pickup by the mortuary squad. Phil was in the bushes with his DS, and then the young sergeant came out ahead of Phil.

Then the mortuary guys were there, and me and my partner were instructed to hold back some of the bushes so the poor woman could be brought out in a body bag.

I held the bush back and I looked at her one last time, then I felt a jolt of electricity run through me. The woman was still looking up at me, but now the opal earrings were gone.

Back in those days, you had to be damn well sure that you were right on the money if you made a complaint against an officer. I had always thought that Phil's DS looked shady, and now with the *earrings gone, I had no doubt he was a thief. How could I prove it? I couldn't. And accusing him would have brought into question Phil's leadership qualities.*

I let it go. It pained me to do so, but I couldn't risk Phil getting into trouble.

The investigation hit high gear after that, with Phil in charge. Every aspect of that young woman's life was checked and double-checked. Nobody questioned the missing earrings. Had nobody noticed she was wearing them? Or maybe they hadn't noticed yet that they were missing. I prepared myself for Phil to be arrested, but he was clever.

A suspect was soon found, an ex-boyfriend. He denied killing the girl, but when they had him in for an interview, he admitted that he had been calling her. He wanted her back. She wasn't interested.

But he had an alibi. Cast iron. We were back to square one. The case went cold.

And then the second victim was found. Another park. Another set of bushes. This woman was a little bit older than the first one, but she had also been dressed up for a night on the town.

This one also had earrings in. Little gold things with what looked like diamonds. Phil was called out again, and once more, hours later, when the body was ready to be picked up, I noticed that the earrings were gone.

I was scared, but I thought I was imagining it. I convinced myself of that, because facing the truth meant that I wouldn't be able to see Phil again, and I was madly in love with the man.

This case went unsolved too. They had two victims killed in the same way, but no clues, no leads, no witnesses. People were getting scared. I remember looking at Phil's DS one day, looked him in the eyes, and at first I thought he was going to snarl and tell me to mind my own business, but he smiled and asked me how I was doing. I saw it then, the charmer, the smiler. The killer. I thought it was him, I really did.

Until the third victim.

This was six months later. I was still seeing Phil. I was falling in love with him.

This woman had been walking home from seeing her boyfriend, who didn't have a car, and I think people were getting complacent by then. This woman took a shortcut through a park and never made it to the other side.

A few boys playing football found her the next day. I was on duty and yes, me and my partner got the call, and she was lying in the bushes, just like the others. I forgot to say – in case you were wondering – no, they weren't sexually assaulted. This was maybe worse than if he had raped them and then killed them. That way, there would have been a motive. What was his motive if he just killed them? He was a psychopath. Which made him more dangerous. Even more dangerous if he was one of us.

Again, the woman wore earrings. Again, they were missing after Phil and his DS checked her over. Why had nobody else noticed? Because they were so busy trying to figure out who the killer was?

I was a lowly WPC – back when it was still okay to call a female officer a Woman Police Officer – and what would I achieve if I went to somebody? It wasn't like today, when you would be listened to. Back then, if you were a female officer, you had to work twice as hard as the men to get up the ladder. Phil Nichol was a highly respected officer who had fought in the war and was a decorated officer. Nobody was going to believe me. Besides, I couldn't prove Phil was taking the earrings.

It did occur to me that he wasn't just taking earrings because they were valuable, he was taking them as trophies.

His wife had taken the two boys to see her mother up in Perth and was going to be staying away for a week. Phil invited me round to his house. I promised myself I wouldn't make love to him in his house, but *promises are meant to be broken, and in that moment in time it felt like I was Mrs Phil Nichol. That this was our house where we lived happily as man and wife.*

We made love twice. I didn't feel ashamed. I was making love to my future husband. Afterwards, I was sitting by the fire in his living room, feeling warm inside and out, when he came into the room with a jewellery box. I thought, this is it! He's going to ask me to marry him; he's going to get rid of the old boot he lives with and we'll be together at last.

But it wasn't an engagement ring. It was a pair of opal earrings.

Mike Holland closed the journal and let his mother's words spin around inside his mind. He'd been told for years just what a bastard his father had been, but if he did indeed kill those women and was never brought to justice for it, then that was a whole new ball game.

He got off the bed and hid the book in his overnight bag. He didn't know how to process this new information, so he didn't try.

Instead, he showered and got ready to have

dinner with Dan O'Brian, which would be fish and chips in the dining room again. The stale smell of the room and the dizzying pattern of the wallpaper made him want to leave right now and just drive back home, but the whisky kicked that idea in the head.

Tomorrow it is then.

FOURTEEN

Harry was in his office, his computer switched on and ready to go. The only problem was, he couldn't get the Zoom thing to work. Christ, he hated computers. He knew they were now an important part of today's society, but they were down there on his list of useless bastard things along with oil protestors and politicians. You knew they were there, and they were a pain in the arse.

Now he was sitting looking at the front page of *The Caledonian* newspaper, digital edition, reading about some wee arseholes who had set fire to a stolen motorbike.

He had read his emails, checked the weather, watched a YouTube video and was about to start reading his horoscope for the day when there was a knock on his office door.

'Come in,' he shouted, but not with any enthusiasm. He'd watched Lillian O'Shea walk in his direction, but she could have been going to the coffee station. Would she ask if he wanted one?

The door opened and he was about to say, thanks and just milk, as if she would have forgotten how he took his coffee since the last time she had made it.

'Neil McGovern just called me, sir. He tried calling you, but his call went straight to voicemail.'

'I know. I switched it off. I took the desk phone off the hook too.'

'Is there a problem? Something I can help you with?'

'Yes, and yes. I was stalling for time.' He looked at his watch: five minutes late for the agreed time to start the conference call. 'I can't get this damned Zoom thing to work. You know me, Lillian; I'm worse than Charlie Skellett when it comes to things like this.'

'I heard that,' Skellett shouted from outside the office door, where his desk was.

'You shouldn't be bloody earwigging.'

'You could have just asked me, Harry. I would have given it a go,' Skellett countered.

'Maybe next time, Charlie,' Lillian said. 'Let me get you joined into the group, sir.'

Lillian walked forward as Harry scooted his chair back. With a few clicks, Harry could see himself as well as Calvin Stewart and Neil McGovern. Lillian clicked something again and Harry's face disappeared, leaving only the other two.

'I have DS Lillian O'Shea here with me helping me fix a bug, but now we've got it worked out. Thanks, Lillian.'

'No problem.' She left his office and closed the door.

'Everything secure?' McGovern asked.

'Check,' Stewart said.

'Yes,' Harry said.

'Right then, I'll get to the point. And this is for your respective ears only. As far as your team is concerned, you're working the case of a murder victim who was in witness protection. I'm trusting you both to keep this confidential.'

Both detectives agreed this would be the case.

'Right then, gentlemen, I'm going to explain how these two murders, one outside Edinburgh and one in Glasgow, are connected. Craig Smith, twenty-six years old. Amanda Brown, twenty-five years old. Boyfriend, girlfriend.

'You may or may not have heard about the case from twelve years ago concerning fifteen-year-old Kevin Tulloch and thirteen-year-old Heather Thom. They were staying at a campsite outside Pitlochry. The families were friends with each other and often went on holiday together. Kevin and Heather were enjoying themselves, and they met another girl there. She was special needs. They didn't know her but decided to bully her.

'Kevin's father was a hunter and had taken his crossbow with him. I don't even know if it was hunting season or not. But anyway, Kevin and Heather took the crossbow, and long story short, they chased this girl into an old caravan dump deep in the woods. It belonged to the campsite. The girl ran into the caravan and was cornered by our two heroes.

'They had her trapped and they got a kick out of seeing her cry. Then Kevin panicked when the girl said she was going to tell her parents. Kevin shot her in the face with an arrow. It went through her mouth and out the side of her neck. She was still alive. Kevin almost collapsed. Heather took the crossbow, put another arrow in it and shot the girl right in the forehead, killing her instantly. They left her there.

'Later on, the girl was reported missing, and a search was started. They found her two hours later.

The arrows were soon traced to Kevin's father, who was the number one suspect, but Kevin broke down and confessed.

'There was public outrage. They wanted Kevin and Heather hanged. But they went to juvenile prison, and when they reached the age of twenty-one, they were given a new identity and put into protection, with the same treatment as witnesses get. Kevin became Craig Smith and Heather became Amanda.'

'I remember that case,' Stewart said.

'Me too,' Harry added.

'I remember they spent millions on keeping those two dirt buckets safe, but that poor lassie's family got nothing,' Stewart said.

'Whatever we think ourselves, we have to ignore our feelings and be professional, Calvin,' McGovern said.

'I know you're right, Neil, but it goes against the grain for me. Those two tossers living in luxury while that poor lassie is deid. It doesn't sit well with me.'

'Let's just focus on this case,' Neil said. 'Somebody found out who they were and executed them. However we feel, it's our job to bring the killer to justice. We need to tread carefully because there's going to be the inevitable comparison, but under no circumstances can their true identities be released to the public.'

'We'll need a list of names of the people who publicly threatened them at the time,' Harry said.

'What about their handlers?' Stewart said. 'They would have been released on licence, so they would have had handlers surely?'

McGovern nodded. 'They did. They were required to check in once a month, and had access to their handlers twenty-four seven. They had checked in earlier in the month and nothing was amiss. I've already spoken to their handlers and they both reported there was nothing amiss.'

'Smith lived in Edinburgh and he was charged with assaulting a co-worker,' Harry said. 'Do you think it could be related?'

'I have my doubts, Harry. If it was just Smith who had been murdered, then yes, I would have gone down that line, but not with both of them being murdered by crossbow. This is related to what they did back then as children. Somebody somewhere found out their true identities and killed them. I want to know how, then we can find out who.'

'Why were they allowed to keep on seeing each

other after they were given new identities?' Stewart asked.

'It was felt there was no harm in it. Smith wasn't too sociable, and he asked if he could keep in touch with Brown. They were given permission.'

'We'll need full access to any old records for the pair,' Stewart said.

'Sorry, no can do. Things have a habit of getting leaked.'

'Offence taken,' Stewart replied.

'What about their parents?' Harry asked.

'In witness protection too. Names changed, new life, new background, the works. They all had slight plastic surgery to alter their looks. You would walk right past them in the street.'

'We're being obstructed here, Neil,' Stewart said.

'It's unfortunate, but that's the way it has to be. Your respective teams can carry out the investigations as if the two victims never had a past. But we'll still liaise with you and can give you some specific information upon request.'

'Who was the arresting officer?' Harry asked.

'A major investigation team were sent from Glasgow as Inverness had their hands full. His name is DI Mike Holland. He's now DCI Holland.'

'What's he got to say for himself?'

'He's on compassionate leave. Due back in Glasgow tomorrow. Calvin, I'd like you to interview him. Take one of your team.'

'How about Lynn McKenzie? You heard about her promotion?'

'I did. She deserved it. Take her along; that will add more weight to it. I just want to get his point of view on this, though. Don't going storming in with jackboots.'

'As if,' Stewart said.

'Any more questions?'

'No,' Stewart said, bordering on sulking like a wee laddie, but Harry knew the big man would be ready to pull somebody's testicles off.

'No,' Harry said.

'Good. I'll be in touch.' McGovern's face disappeared from the screen.

'I'll be in touch, Harry,' Stewart said. 'I'll stay through here for a little while. You're in charge in my absence. Talk to you later, son.'

Stewart was the next to disappear.

'Christ, how do you get out of this monstrosity?' Harry said out loud. Then he waved to Lillian, who smiled at him and came back over.

'Still getting lippy with you, boss?' she asked, nodding to the machine.

'It is. Cheeky wee bastard that it is.' He moved out of Lillian's way while she shut his meeting down.

'You know, Lillian, they say that AI and robots will take over the world. I think that's a load of pish, if this bloody thing's anything to go by.'

'You should still keep an eye on the kettle, boss. You never know.' She laughed as she left the office.

FIFTEEN

Mike Holland decided to walk along to his mother's house. The fresh air would do him good, although he had never been a fan of fresh air before. Glasgow air with fumes from the buses was what he was used to.

He walked to the top of the road and took a right, heading along to his mother's street, which was only five minutes away by foot. It had got colder and the sun was barely hanging on to the day, like it was standing by the machine, waiting to clock out.

He didn't know if Maggie would still be in the house or not, but it wasn't like he was there to break into the house. The car was gone, he noticed. That was an easy sell, and the price the priest had paid had to be above market value. He would check online later, just out of curiosity.

The Baxters had a light on behind their curtains, even though the last of the daylight was still with them. Maybe it was for old man Baxter to be able to polish his chainsaw.

Holland took the key out and let himself into the house. He closed the curtains at the front and switched a lamp on. Maggie had been busy filling bin liners with his mother's stuff. She had left the living room things in the living room, which made it easy to find the bedroom contents.

He stood in silence for a moment, seeing his little girls in his mind's eye, running about the living room, running from room to room. His mother sitting with a cup of tea, probably laced with some form of alcohol. He could hear her voice in his head as clear as if he had just spoken to her yesterday.

Then a red flashing light caught his eye. Her answering machine. He walked over to it and hit the play button.

'You're a little bastard, you know that?' Dear old Uncle Richard, being a dick again.

'You think I came up to my sister's house to fucking chorie stuff? Is that what you think of me? You won't sully my fucking name. You should have stayed out of her life. Everybody was so much happier when you weren't around.'

End of message.

Holland shook his head. He knew when he saw Dick at the funeral that would be the last time he would ever clap eyes on him.

Holland walked through to the bedroom, where Helen's clothes had been bagged. The other things hadn't been touched yet, the trinkets on the chest of drawers, the small figurines.

The jewellery box.

He looked at it for a moment as if it were Pandora's box itself. It was small, about eight inches wide, and made of a light wood. Bamboo maybe. Holland wasn't up on what different trees looked like when they were cut down and shaped into boxes.

He reached a hand out and touched it. The lid was smooth and shiny like she had kept it polished. It had a little clasp on the front. He got a fingernail underneath it and lifted, but it lifted the whole box. He put a hand on top and tried again.

This time it opened. There were a few neck chains on top, cheap earrings. He lifted the top layer and looked inside. Looked into the abyss.

'Are you sure you don't want to do the eulogy yourself?' Dan O'Brian said just as Sam came into the room with the fish suppers.

'Here we go, lads,' he said, putting the packages on plates and putting them in front of the two men.

'Thanks, Sam,' Holland said. 'Put this on my bill, will you?'

'Och, away, man. This is on me.'

'Very good of you, Sammy old son,' the priest said, tearing into the wrapper like there was gold inside. 'I have to say, I'm starving. I've been watching my weight, cutting out carbs and sugar. I almost feel like I could run to the car now if it started pelting down.'

Sam sat down at the table. He had brought in bottles of Irn-Bru as well. 'Cheers,' he said after he'd opened his.

'Here's to us,' Holland said, taking the cap off his plastic bottle and knocking it against the landlord's.

'Here's to the memory of our friend Helen,' O'Brian said.

'Have you heard back from the funeral director yet?' Sam asked, tucking into his fish.

'No, it's too soon. We have to make sure there's a slot for her, but I'm sure it won't be long,' Holland said. His feelings of sadness had turned into...what?

He wasn't sure. Not hatred. Disappointment? Yes, there was certainly disappointment. Maybe a twinge of fear, although he couldn't explain that one.

'I wish we could be there for you, pal, but you know how it is with running your own business,' Sam said.

'I understand,' Holland said after washing down a piece of fish.

'Cheryl and I will be there in spirit, though. And you'll be in good hands with the father here.'

'Amen,' O'Brian said.

They chatted more for a while, then Sam excused himself.

'Did Helen ever go into detail about your father?' O'Brian asked. 'I mean, real detail?'

Holland thought about his answer for a moment. 'No. Not really. Why?'

'I want you to find peace, Mike. If you wanted to bat anything off me, I'm obviously a good listener.'

He smiled at the man he now called his friend. 'I appreciate that. But Helen just wanted me to know how bad my father was so I'd get that he was never going to be around or take any interest in me.'

'Have you heard any more from your brothers?'

'I'm going to meet Walter tomorrow. Hugh's having a hard time with this new family stuff. It came as a shock to him to find out his old man was having it away with another lassie. However, I wish I had done something about meeting them years ago.'

'You'll be fine.'

Holland cleared away the plates and the fish wrappers, taking them through to the kitchen, where he cleaned the plates while O'Brian watched.

'What about you, Dan? Any family?'

O'Brian was leaning against the doorframe of the kitchen. 'My father died a long time ago. My mother recently died. I have no siblings.' He stood up straight. 'Who needs siblings when you have a couple of dozen members of a flock who come to visit every Sunday without fail?'

'That's true. Less Christmas presents too. Win-win.'

'What about you, Mike? Any siblings?'

Holland turned to look at the priest as he rinsed the dishes. 'No. I did have a sister, but she died a long time ago.'

'Sorry to hear that.'

'Don't be. We were never close. My adoptive mother had already adopted her by the time I came along. I hadn't seen her in a very long time.' He turned back to the sink. 'Who needs families anyway? They're just too complicated.'

'Remember, they're only complicated if you let them be. Like your uncle; he's upset at you, but it goes deeper than that. It sounds like he resented your mother for going out and having a good time. It sounds like he was oppressed.'

Holland finished the dishes and dried his hands. 'Maybe you've got a point.'

They walked to the front door and Holland opened it for the priest. He saw his mother's car outside and remembered he would have to cash the cheque.

'How's she running?' he asked.

'Not too bad. Maybe a little tune-up and an oil change and she'll be right as rain. Maybe stretching her legs on the way down to Glenrothes will help her too.'

They shook hands.

'Thanks for everything you've done for me,' Holland said.

'No problem. I'll see you at the funeral.'

'See you then.'

After Holland closed the door, he felt exhausted, and he was climbing the stairs to go to his room when he got a call.

'Hello?' he said, slowly taking each step.

'You don't know me, DCI Holland, but my

name's Neil McGovern. I work for the Scottish government. I need you to report to Helen Street at ten o'clock tomorrow for an informal chat with Detective Chief Superintendent Lynn McKenzie.'

Holland felt there was something suspicious about the call. 'Listen, I don't know who you are, pal, but Lynn McKenzie isn't a DCS.'

'She is now.'

'Yeah, well, I don't know where you got this number. Are you with Standards?'

'No, I'm not with Professional Standards. I just told you.'

'If you were genuine, you would know why I won't be in Helen Street tomorrow. Call me again and you'll find out just how far my arms reach. Dickhead.'

He hung up and immediately blocked the number. God knows who his uncle had got to make the phone call to wind him up, but he needed to do better. Just another thing he was going to have a talk with the old man about.

He got into his room and locked the door and took his shoes off before taking his mother's journal out. He reached into his pocket and took out the opal earrings.

He sat on the bed and opened the journal.

SIXTEEN

Harry sat in his office reading through the Craig Smith and Amanda Brown file. It was getting late, time to start wrapping up for the day, but he was frustrated by this case. They were being hobbled by Neil McGovern, who was very much playing his cards close to his chest.

He looked through the office window and saw his wife, DS Alex McNeil, come into the incident room. He got up out of his chair, feeling his arse was going numb.

'Look at this, it's the better-looking McNeil,' Charlie Skellett said. He was eating a Rich Tea, dunking it into his mug of tea, trying to time it so it wouldn't get too soggy and fall in.

'Thank you for that, Charlie,' Alex said.

'No problem, miss. I'm here to please. Grab a pew and I'll make you a cup of tea.'

'I'm fine, thanks. I don't want to be peeing all night.'

'I hear you. I have a cut-off at seven in the evening. Nothing to eat or drink after the witching hour, as my wife calls it.'

'That's the best thing for losing weight. However, it's past dinnertime and I'm starving. I'm that hungry, I'd even consider eating one of those things.' She pointed to the packet of biscuits.

'Rich Tea get a bad rep.'

'Hi, Alex,' Lillian said. Elvis waved, as did Julie.

'Hi, folks. Good to see you again.' Alex looked around for Frank Miller, but he was nowhere to be seen.

'How's Fife treating you?' Lillian said.

'I'm enjoying it over there. Max Hold is a good guy to work with.'

'Should I be getting jealous?' Harry said as he came from his office into the incident room.

'Absolutely you should,' she said, smiling.

'I knew it.' He walked over to the kettle. 'Anybody want one?'

'Got one, thanks, chief,' Skellett said. 'Your

163

missus mentioned something about bladder problems, so that will be a no for her.'

'Charlie!' Alex said. 'You're making me think I'm as old as you.'

'Don't knock it; some people don't get to my age.' He laughed and carried on dunking and slurping.

'How's your leg doing?' she asked him.

'Still the same, hen. The doc doesn't want to go in laparoscopically and play around. He says he could make things worse, but how much worse could it be? I just want to be able to walk properly again.'

'Hopefully, it will heal on its own.'

'Fingers crossed.'

Harry walked over to the whiteboard as he waited for the kettle to boil.

'Calvin is just as much in the dark with his victim as we are,' he said to the others. 'Amanda Brown was Craig Smith's girlfriend, but they had history. I can't go into all the details, but they went way back.'

'They killed a wee lassie with a crossbow twelve years ago,' Skellett said.

Harry turned to look at him. 'You never heard that from me.'

'I know I didn't. I know there's a news blackout on the victims, but we know Smith was shot with a crossbow, and I'm going out on a limb here, but I'm willing to bet his girlfriend was killed in the same way. I haven't heard from Calvin, but I *did* look online, and what came up was that case from twelve years ago where that pair killed a wee lassie in a caravan. They were put in juvenile and released under licence when they were twenty-one. Millions were spent giving them new identities. Good to see how they spend our tax money, protecting those little bastards. I'm guessing now that somebody found out who they were and took care of them in the same way as they killed their victim. Am I right, Harry? The victim in Glasgow is Heather Thom and our boy is Kevin Tulloch. Their original names.'

Harry drew in a breath and blew it out.

'Christ, Neil McGovern will have my bloody neck in a sling if he thinks I told you their names.'

'Get him to call me then, and I'll introduce him to Google. He's daft if he thinks we wouldn't make the connection. We're detectives after all.'

Harry looked at them all in turn. 'Listen to me right now. If McGovern thinks you're going behind his back and playing around with two of his protectees, you'll be finished in MIT. You'll be lucky if you get booted down back to uniform. McGovern wields a lot of power.'

'It won't leave this room, Harry. My lips are sealed,' Skellett said.

'How about the rest of you? Fancy directing traffic in the Outer Hebrides?'

'No, it won't leave this room,' Lillian said, and Julie and Elvis agreed that it might not be as much fun chasing a tractor in a country lane as it was working here in Edinburgh.

'Right then. You're right, Charlie. They were put into witness protection; even though they weren't technically witnesses to anything, they fell under that umbrella. Somebody found out their true identities and killed them. This is going to be one of our hardest cases because there are no witnesses, no leads, nothing. But we have to work it until we get a lead. Alex?'

She looked at her husband. 'Yes?'

'Liaise with uniform. Have them go back round the houses near where Smith lived. Somebody might have seen something. Check on the houses where nobody answered first time.'

'Will do.'

Harry looked at Skellett. 'Have you heard from Frank at all?'

Skellett shook his head. 'He was away chasing down family members of Smith's assault victim.'

'Call him and tell him to call it a day. We can debrief tomorrow. Time to get home, I think.'

They closed up for the night, each of them going their own way.

Out in the car park, Harry walked Alex over to her car. 'Did you call Jessica?' Alex's sister and their babysitter.

'She's giving Grace her dinner.'

'I feel knackered,' he told her.

'Oh, and here was me planning a night of wild romance.'

'I didn't say I was incapable,' Harry said.

'Let's see after dinner, shall we, Romeo?' She laughed as she got into her car.

SEVENTEEN

'I swear to God, my eyeballs have been seared. I can't even see properly,' DS Robbie Evans said, turning the car into the street they had visited earlier. The forensics team were still here and some uniforms, keeping an eye on things.

'What are you gibbering on about now, Robbie? Did you see your auld maw in her underwear or something?' DCI Jimmy Dunbar said from the passenger seat.

'Seeing Hamish with his trousers round his ankles. Scarred me for life, it has.'

'Don't talk shite. I can see you weren't in the army. We had to shower with other men.'

'That's alright for you to say, you didn't see the

bastard's tadger. Flapping about in the wind, poking out from its ginger rat's nest. I thought I was going to puke.'

'And Angie Fisher saw it as well. I bet she took photos just so she can blackmail the wee bastard in the future.'

'Wouldn't surprise me.'

'I'll tell her that, will I?'

Evans pulled the car in behind Calvin Stewart's. 'Maybe not. She'd kick the crap out of me.'

'She would that, son.'

'Oh Christ, here's Calvin now.'

They got out into the dark. The air was icy, like a good belting of snow was just around the corner.

'This is shite,' Stewart said. 'Not one of those shiftless bastards saw anything. Aye, right. I've got a good mind to get a drug-sniffing dug down here and have at it. You know what I told one of those fuckers?'

Dunbar looked at Evans, trying to coax him to have first go at guessing, but the younger DS just stood there like a right glaikit bastard.

'You told him that you'd boot him round the bollocks?' Dunbar guessed.

'It was a woman, but I told her, we have reason to

believe this bastard is targeting people who live round here.' Stewart laughed. 'That soon changed her story. She looked like a ferret had just climbed into her tights. I told her that we wouldn't be able to protect them, but if she saw something then she needs to speak up. Her and all the fucking rest of them round here. She told me she'd seen somebody creeping about near Amanda Brown's stair.'

'Let me guess, she didn't give a description?' Evans said.

'She did, actually. Well, not down to the last hair on his bollocks, but she said he was a big guy, short hair, drove a red hatchback.'

Angie Fisher came walking down a pathway from one of the tenement stairs and joined them.

'Any luck?' Stewart asked her.

She looked like she had been sitting too close to an electric fire, her cheeks taking the brunt of it.

'Actually, yes. Whatever you said to that bloke wearing the dress, it worked. Word must have got round that they were all going to die in their beds tonight.'

'See? I told you there was something fishy about that bastard.'

'It's acceptable for men to wear dresses nowadays, sir,' Evans said.

'Is that right? You wear your ma's dress at the weekends?'

'No, no, I mean with all this trans movement, men feel more relaxed about who they are and aren't afraid to show it.'

'You're trying to goad me into saying some shite that isn't PC nowadays, aren't you?'

'Not at all, sir.'

'Well, don't just stand there, go and find Gingy Baws. I'm sure he'll be pleased to see you since you got his trousers down on the first date.'

'That's hilarious, sir.' Evans walked away to find Hamish so they could compare notes.

Angie laughed. 'Poor guys. I don't know which one of them was more embarrassed.'

'He knows I'm just pulling his tadger. As it were,' Stewart said. 'But what did you find out?'

'Somebody else saw the red hatchback. It was a Vauxhall. They didn't get the plate, though.'

'That would have been the icing on the cake,' Dunbar said. 'We'll keep on talking to them, see if we can find somebody else who saw this car.'

'I assumed that they would be able to spot a strange car here, and I was right,' Angie said. 'It's like they've got their own wee neighbourhood watch thing going on.'

Hamish came out of another stair and walked quickly towards the group of detectives.

'Keep hold of your fucking troosers there,' Stewart said. Hamish stopped for a moment, then shook his head and approached them.

'I spoke to a guy in one of those flats. He says he got the plate number.'

'Is it true?' Stewart asked. 'You were flashing on the job? I could place you under arrest right now for that.'

Hamish pulled a beamer. 'Not exactly. I had a wardrobe malfunction, that's all. It was immediately corrected and I carried on with my duties.'

'He's winding you up, Hamish,' Angie said, smiling at him.

'Oh, right. Good one, sir.'

'Just make sure you keep them up from now on. None of this branching out on your own.' Stewart grinned and nudged Angie. 'Get it?'

'Will do,' Hamish said.

'Right then, lead me to this witness, and if it turns out to be a pile of pish, one of you is getting a boot in the bollocks.'

'Don't boot the messenger,' Dunbar said.

'Aye, we'll see. Now lead the way, son. Meantime, you lot keep canvassing. Angie, with me.'

Hamish walked in front of the two senior detectives, walking them into the stair. The witness lived on the ground floor. A uniform stood at the stair door, while another was walking about with a police dog. The German Shepherd growled at Stewart, then started barking.

'Easy, ya fucking bellend,' the handler said, yanking back on the dog's harness.

Stewart thought the man was talking to him at first. 'Keep that fucking thing on a tight lead,' he warned. 'You don't want to know what will happen if it bites me.'

The man took the dog away.

'He's in there, sir. Malcolm Dunn.'

Stewart walked into the lobby, where a bare bulb dangled from a cord, making it look like they were in some cheap underground nightclub where wee underage gadgies drank and smoked and pretended they were hard.

The carpet smelled, like Dunn had a dog, or somebody had, and didn't run a carpet cleaner over it. The walls were covered in council woodchip wallpaper which once upon a time had been a magnolia colour, but the tenant had added dirt and scrapes to it, adding his own personal touch. It looked like somebody had picked at a seam, maybe thinking about stripping it to put something new on, but had then thought it was going to be too much like hard work and had abandoned the idea.

'He's in here, sir,' Hamish said, indicating the living room with the same flourish that a magician's assistant might use.

Stewart and Angie walked in after him.

Hamish turned round and lowered his voice in front of the tenant. 'He's a midget,' he said.

'Hey! I fucking heard that,' Malcolm Dunn said. 'And it's small. Ignorant bastard.'

'Sorry,' Hamish said, keeping his voice low. 'Small midget.'

'I think you're just taking the fucking piss now,' Dunn said. He had jumped up onto his settee, where his legs sank into the old cushions, like he was wanting a square go with the ginger bastard.

'Right, son, get out,' Stewart said, and he and Angie stepped aside to let the DC leave.

'Christ,' Stewart said when O'Connor was gone. Then to Dunn: 'You can come off that now.'

Dunn ignored him for a second. 'I heard a big dug outside. I don't like dugs. They think I'm a dug toy.'

'My colleague said you had something to tell us?' Angie said.

'Like I'm telling you anything now after Rolf fucking Harris called me a midget.'

'Rolf Harris wasn't ginger,' Stewart said.

'Aye well, *he* looks like the ginger version of Rolf Harris.'

'You mean my DC is a good painter?' Stewart said.

'Put whatever fucking spin you want on it, mate.'

Stewart turned to Angie. 'Tell the dog handler to bring his dug in here so it can sniff around.'

Dunn screamed, 'Not without a warrant, you can't!'

'Probable cause, son. I smell weed in here. What about you, DCI Fisher?'

'Absolutely. I'm almost getting high off the smell.'

'It's either that or you spilled a tandoori on your carpet. My money's on the weed. What say you, DCI Fisher?'

'Definitely weed.'

'It's medicinal!' Dunn shouted as Angie made her way out into the lobby.

'The dug might find some other interesting stuff. I heard that it can sniff out porn on a computer too.'

'Och, away ye go. Fucking sniff porn indeed.'

'That didn't sound like a denial to me, wee man.'

'Don't call me wee man.'

'Because of the actor? Oh, okay, big man.'

'Fuck you.'

'Angie!' Stewart shouted. 'Where's the boy with the big dug?'

'Alright, alright,' Dunn said, jumping off the settee with an agility that surprised Stewart. He sat down.

'Never mind!' Stewart shouted.

Angie walked back into the room and they could all hear the police dog somewhere close by, giving a disappointed bark that he hadn't sunk his teeth into somebody's arse.

'You want a cup of tea or anything?' Dunn asked, his attitude now one of compliance. 'I might have some biscuits.'

'Shortbread?' Stewart said.

'You're hilarious. Rich Tea. And I licked them all.'

'You're fine, Malky. You don't mind if I call you Malky, do you?' Stewart said. He looked towards the living room door as if the dog handler was hiding out in the lobby waiting to shout 'Get the bastard!' or whatever command it was they used.

'Better than "Shorty". Trust me, I've been called everything under the sun. But let me tell you, I still get my end away.'

'Alright, Mr Dunn, I'm sure DSup Stewart isn't interested in your sex life,' Angie said.

'How about you then?'

'I'll pass, thanks.'

'You and I could have a good time together.' Dunn suddenly found a new confidence. 'Or don't you date little people?'

'I'm married,' she answered. Technically, she *was* still married, as the divorce hadn't been finalised.

'How about you, big man?' Dunn said. 'You and me could hit the town. We would pull no problem.'

'I'm already spoken for, manky wee bastard. If you don't shut your fucking hole, not only will I call the handler, but we'll all stand out in the fucking lobby and lock you in here with Rin Tin Tin.'

Dunn tutted. 'See what I get for trying to be friendly? I thought we were connecting on a different level.' He looked at both detectives. 'I'm not like those other scally bastards. I work.'

Stewart silently looked at Angie, wondering if she was going to blurt out something about the circus, but she sat quietly.

'Where do you work?' Stewart asked, sitting down on a chair.

'I work in a bakery. I make the holes in the doughnuts. Guess what with?'

'Oh God,' Angie said.

Dunn laughed. 'I do work in a bakery, though. I want to open my own one day. I'm a pretty good baker. I have some rolls you can take away with you if you like?' He beamed a smile at Angie as he slipped off the settee and left the room. Stewart was confident that the uniform at the door would be enough of a deterrent should the small man try to make a run for it.

Dunn didn't run, he just went to the kitchen and brought back some rolls in a Ziploc bag.

'I made them with my own hands.' He handed them over to Angie.

'You've not laced them with anything I hope,' Stewart said.

Dunn sat back down. 'I'm offended.'

'This place fucking honks of you smoking weed, so forgive me if I was wondering if you had added your special ingredient to your rolls.'

Dunn waved him away. 'I only smoke the stuff; I don't make brownies.' He looked between them again. 'I'm serious. I'm proud of my work. You'll see, I'll have my own bakery one day: Midge's Bakery.'

'You what?' Stewart said.

'Midge is my middle name, after Midge Ure. My mum loved him.'

'It sounds like Midget's Bakery, if you don't mind me saying so,' Angie said.

'Come again?'

Stewart nodded. 'Imagine people are going home pished and you have your bakery open and they're piling in because your stuff is so good; they'll say, let's go to Midget's Bakery. Sorry to pish on your parade, son, but if you want my advice, stick with Dunn's. How about Dunn and Dusted? You know, the rolls are done, then dusted with flour.'

Dunn leaned forward a bit. 'That's bloody good! Mind if I pinch it?'

'Help yourself.'

Dunn smiled to himself. 'You can have free rolls for life,' he said.

'Right then, Malky, back to business if you don't mind, son. You saw something the night Amanda Brown was murdered?'

'Aye, I did. There was some big bloke hanging around outside her stair door for a minute.'

Stewart wondered if the man had indeed been big, or did an average-sized man just *seem* big to Dunn?

'Anyway, I was going out to work – I start at four-thirty in the a.m. – and I clocked him. He looked like he had been in shagging somebody and was looking to see if the coast was clear before booting off. He walked to his car and got in. Now, I admit, I'm a nosy bastard at the best of times. You have to be round here. I'd like to live in Bearsden one day, but I know I have to work up to that. This is a shitehole, so I'm always wary. Some people are just coming home when I'm going out to work. I got into my car and as the car passed with the big man in it, I had my phone out; I was about to plug it into the charger. So I snapped off a couple of photos.'

'Did you get his face?' Stewart asked.

'I'm good, but I'm not that good. I got a photo of the plate, though.' Dunn took his phone out and opened the photos and showed a clear photo of the licence plate on the red hatchback.

'Can I take a photo of your photo?' Angie asked.

'Go ahead.' Dunn angled the phone towards Angie and she took a photo. Then they both put their phones away.

She stood up and left the room, going to call the control centre and have them run the plate.

'Thanks, Malky, you've been a great help,' Stewart said. He stood up and Dunn did the same. 'Listen, pal, I'm sorry about being a smartarse there. I hope you get your bakery one day.'

'Ach, it's just a pipe dream.'

'Not if you work hard enough.' Stewart took his business card out and passed it over to the man. 'If you ever need some advice, I know people. But where do you work just now?'

'Bud's Bakery, over on Elderpark Street.'

'Christ, I've been in there. Good stuff.'

'I rest my case.' Dunn smiled at him.

'See you around, pal.' Stewart left the flat and met Angie outside. She was still clutching the bag of rolls.

'You going to eat them?' Stewart asked.

'What do you think?'

'Give them to me. I'll risk it for a biscuit.'

'Did you bang your head or something?'

'I think that despite him being a wee smartarse, he's genuine. I like him.'

'What's not to like? He's still not my type, though, before you ask.'

'Aye, I noticed you lying to him about being married.'

'Not for much longer. My ex can't wait to get rid of me so he can tie the knot with that wee hoor he's going with.' Angie shook her head. 'Anyway, I know who the car belongs to.'

'Can we pick the bastard up tonight?' Stewart asked.

'We'll never be able to pick him up. It belongs to Craig Smith.'

EIGHTEEN

A glass of whisky by his side on the bedside cabinet and a muted light coming from the little lamp, Holland stared at the black ink his mother had used to write her words. Her handwriting was clear. It was obvious that she hadn't wanted any words to be misunderstood.

He started reading.

Things calmed down. The murders went unsolved, and Phil worked hard. He told me they were hitting a brick wall with the investigation, and I started to have doubts. Serious doubts. Maybe the opal earrings were ones he bought. Yes, I convinced myself that they only looked like the ones that were on the victim.

I was head over heels in love with your father. Christmas Day 1962, I wanted to see Phil. I was living with my mum and dad, and my brother and sister. Richard was being his usual pain-in-the-arse self, and after dinner he said he was going to spend time with his pals. My sister was busy stuffing her face with cake – the fat cow! – and I lied to my parents. I told them I was working the back shift.

Phil and I had a plan. His wife and kids were going to her mother's. He told her he was feeling ill, so she went by herself. I got my uniform on and went round to his house where we...well, you know. I was twenty-one by this time and had been seeing Phil for a couple of years. Off and on. I think we had a clash of personalities. We were really like oil and water, but when we were good, we were good. I knew I loved him and was willing to wait. That was what I told him, and by that Christmas, I had been waiting for two years.

That Christmas Eve, we had been working together. He said he would try and tell his wife that he was leaving her, and I told him that would be the best Christmas present he could ever give me.

I couldn't care less if he was ripping his family

apart. Is that bad of me? I don't care. Means to an end and all that. If she wasn't such a dowdy bitch, he might not have looked for love elsewhere. He had me – young, fit and would do anything for him.

I went round that Christmas Day expecting to have an engagement ring on by the time Boxing Day crept in at midnight. I was staying over (I had already told your grandad and granny that I was spending the night with one of my girlfriends, so they weren't expecting me home). I was more than excited, let me tell you.

Things started off fine. We had a nice meal, had a drink and then we went through to the bedroom. I'll spare you the details, ha! But you're a big boy, Mike. Fill in the blanks.

We were lying in bed, smoking and drinking, waiting for Phil's clock to reset, if you know what I mean. I asked him flat out how the conversation had gone when he told his wife he was leaving her.

He looked at me then, looked me right in the fucking eyes, and told me he hadn't gone through with it. He didn't want to spoil Christmas for the kids. He waited until he had fucked me before telling me this! Now do you see what an absolute bastard he was?

I jumped out of bed and got dressed. He was trying to placate me, but I wasn't listening to him.

Then the phone rang and I thought it was his wife, so I answered it. He tried to stop me, but I was so angry. I said 'Hello?' and this young woman was on the phone, and she asked to speak to him. I told her I was a colleague of his and said, 'Can I ask who's calling?' Phil meantime was hopping about like a sparrow, trying to get his pants and trousers on.

The woman said, 'I'm a friend of his.' I knew then that she was just another girlfriend of his. I hung up on her and told Phil we were finished.

It was six weeks later that I found out I was pregnant with you.

Of course, he was hopping mad. He told me to get rid of you. Said I couldn't possibly keep you. But I told him there was no way on earth I was getting rid of you. We argued a lot after that, and I think he was hoping I would have a miscarriage, but I didn't.

I went down to Edinburgh to have you. I took maternity leave from the force, with a promise that I was going back. The main reason I went away was shame. Not for me, I couldn't care less, but my mum and dad were appalled. They were more ashamed than appalled to be honest, and they said I should go away to have 'the bastard child' as my mother put it.

And then I was to give you away. Nobody wanted you around; not my parents, not Phil, not anybody except me. It was like water trying to run uphill. I was getting it from every side. I caved, that's what happened.

Phil came with me to the adoption agency in Edinburgh, where everything was arranged. I'd have you in the nuns' home for unwed mothers. Phil was in the background and wouldn't answer many questions from the agency.

I went into the home, which was just round the corner from Simpson's Memorial Maternity Hospital in Lauriston. They've built flats there now, after pulling it down. The home I was in was a very old building. There were six of us in one room, all at various stages of pregnancy. It was like a boarding house in Blackpool, people coming and going all the time. I didn't see your father once in all that time, but I called him and he took my calls.

At the end of September, you arrived, and I had to give you up six weeks later. I went back to my old life, my old job, my old everything. Phil was cool towards me and I heard a rumour he had found another girl-friend, but he refused to talk about it. However, a week after I arrived back, we got together. It was wonderful. Now I felt like things were back to normal.

Then I got a shout one night. A young woman

found dead in a park. It was starting all over again. Once again, Phil and his team were called out, and I swear, I had a look to see if the woman had earrings in and she didn't. She was wearing a bracelet, though, a gold band with some kind of fake stones in it. It looked pretty, and I made sure in my mind it was there before Phil got there.

After everybody had been to see her and deal with her, the mortuary men came to take her away. I made sure I had a look at her before she was put on the stretcher and guess what? The bracelet was gone.

I braced myself this time. Phil took me to dinner one night. His wife was off visiting some family member or other, and we went to a quiet restaurant in Glenrothes. Well away from Dunfermline. At the table, he reached into his pocket and brought out a velvet box. Not ring size but bigger. Inside was the bracelet. It had been cleaned and shone in the dull light of the restaurant, but I knew it was hers.

The woman he'd killed.

I was shaking. I was accepting jewellery from a serial killer, something a dead woman once wore. I took it, not because I wanted it but because I was scared not to.

You're probably thinking, what the hell, Helen? You knew he killed women, but you still wanted to be with him? Why didn't you dump him? Why didn't you go to your superior officers if he was a killer?

I knew I should do both things, but you never met your father. You never got to see the charming side of him, the loving, caring side of him. Besides, I had absolutely no proof he was a killer. The jewellery? I had that in my possession but couldn't prove he'd given it to me.

I went through a period of depression, a time when I didn't see Phil much. I wanted you back. I went to speak to Phil and told him there was a grace period where I could change my mind and take you back, before you were formally adopted. I wanted Phil to be on board, to finally see my point of view; we could get you back and start a new life together.

But he said no, of course.

I saw him out in the pub one night with another WPC; I knew her from work. I thought my life with Phil was over and sank into a deeper depression.

I poured myself into my work, and then one day we got a call for another victim. This one wasn't found in a park but in a small flat on the outskirts of Dunfermline. This time there was a manhunt on. The victim was a police officer. Friends of the woman said she had a new boyfriend, but nobody knew who he was.

Mike, I was scared then. Phil turned up and I'd never seen him look so pale. He didn't get angry, didn't show emotion, kept it very professional. He was such a fucking good actor! I am gripping the pen so hard as I write this, I am so angry.

I knew this woman was his other girlfriend, the woman who had been in the pub with him. Again, I didn't have proof. This was the early sixties, and not every man and his dog had a video camera in his pocket. I can only say that I suspected she was his girlfriend.

The investigation hit high gear, but you know what's coming now, don't you? Nobody was ever arrested for the murder. Phil got away with it again. This time, I didn't see anything go missing. Her body was taken away by the mortuary men and she still had her earrings in.

Yes, I should have stopped then. Should have told Phil, if you're not going to marry me, then we're done. But I didn't.

Instead, our affair carried on through the years, me hoping that one day I would be the new Mrs Nichol, but I never was.

It didn't stop me getting pregnant, though. In the spring of 1968, I gave birth to your little brother,

David. He had a heart defect and he died after a few weeks.

Phil was beside himself. I'd told him I wasn't running away to Edinburgh this time, and he'd begged me not to stay in Dunfermline and have the baby. He paid for me to live in a little flat in St Andrews, and I had the baby in Craigtoun Maternity Hospital. David was transferred to Dundee, where he died.

I returned to Dunfermline, only to find Phil had moved on once again. I thought I could rekindle things, not fully aware that we had broken up since I was carrying his child! But then I saw he was with somebody else.

Somebody he had left his wife and kids for.

That was Phil and me finally over.

So you see, Mike, your father was a complicated man. I was expecting to hear that he had killed this girlfriend too, but he never did. And I resigned from the force.

Holland sat back in the bed and grabbed the whisky glass. He chugged the golden liquid back in one go, the burning sensation feeling good.

His mother had been dating a serial killer and she'd thought he was a bastard, yet almost five years after she'd had Holland, she'd had another child with his father, a child who'd died.

Holland shook his head.

'He couldn't have been that bad, eh, Helen?' he said out loud. 'You kept going back to him. Why would you do that if he was so bad?'

He closed the journal and poured himself another whisky.

NINETEEN

Neil McGovern sat at the restaurant table opposite his daughter, Kim Miller. It was an Italian place in the High Street, just around the corner from where Kim lived.

'You could have swept your offices for bugs,' Kim said, taking a sip of her white wine.

'It's not bugs I'm worried about, it's people.' McGovern shook his head. 'What's the world coming to when you can't trust the people who work under you?' He took a sip of his lager. It was cold and hit the spot.

'It might not be anybody in the department,' Kim said.

'That's why I'm having an investigator come in from outside.'

'You are?'

'Yes, I am. And here he is. Miles Tate. I've heard good things about him.'

'Never heard of him.'

McGovern stood up as a tall man approached. He was in his mid-thirties, hair cut short, wore the prerequisite five o'clock shadow for posers every-where. Tate loved himself. Women loved him too, and he knew it.

'Miles, thanks for coming up so quickly. We've never met, but I've heard good things about you. This is my daughter, Kim Miller.'

'Pleased to meet you, Kim.' Tate smiled at her.

'Likewise.'

'How's life in London?'

'Smelly as always.' He smiled, showing a set of teeth that he'd spent a fortune on. They weren't real but weren't falsers in the traditional sense.

'That's one thing I don't miss about the place. I much prefer the Scottish air.'

McGovern indicated for the young man to sit and he complied.

'Wine?' Kim asked.

'Not when I'm working, thanks.'

Tate wore an expensive suit, the kind made by little men who thought nothing of coming into close contact with your bollocks. His shirt looked sharp and his tie was made of silk with a subtle but elegant pattern that expensive wallpapers couldn't hold a candle to.

'I took the liberty of ordering you spaghetti and meatballs. They're the best. I knew you were on your way over, so they won't be long in coming out.'

'Terrific, thank you.'

'Miles old son, I hate to get right down to business, but what have you got for me?'

'Where do I start?' Tate said. 'Two of your staff are having an affair, one is unhappy in his work and is about to give in his notice, and the others are plodding along.'

'You got all of this from their computers?' Kim said.

'Yes. There's nowhere to hide on those machines, and they make the mistake of using the company emails to talk to each other and write things down. But that's all there is to tell. There are no bugs. My team went in and swept the place. The bank accounts of your team members don't show any irregularities. I would say you have a clean office there. Wherever your leak came from, it wasn't internal.'

'Then where the hell did it come from?'

Even though it was early evening, they were still

working. 'Somebody had to have leaked the information on the outside,' Kim said.

'I agree,' Tate said. 'I've already started running checks on prison employees, both current and former, to get an idea of their background. Just in case. And I'm checking both Tulloch's and Thom's employers just now. Tulloch worked in Edinburgh until the assault scandal, then he moved through to Fife, where he lived. I'm having one of my team go through the employer's system tonight.'

'Good work, Miles.'

Their food arrived and they automatically started talking about trivial things while the waiter served their food.

'Two of my clients are dead and I want to know who took them out,' McGovern said when the waiter had gone.

'We should be looking at somebody for a revenge killing,' Kim said.

'The mother of their victim died of cancer two years ago. The father moved on, got married and moved to London,' McGovern said.

'This is good,' Tate said, tucking in. After he'd swallowed, he wiped his face with his napkin. 'I had the father checked out; he had a stroke a couple of months ago. He's been going to physiotherapy and his movements can be accounted for. I mean, he could have hired somebody of course, but he couldn't physically do it himself. What are the chances he found out who they were now and where they lived? Slim to none. I had one of my team go through his social media posts and there's been nothing indicating he wanted to find them or even talking about them. It could be a smokescreen, but you know yourselves, there's usually something that gives them away. This guy has moved on, remarried, got a decent job. My opinion is, he's not the one.'

'Good job, son,' McGovern said. 'I thought it was a long shot, but we can keep an open mind on him. Meantime, somebody found out who Tulloch and Thom were, so we can go down any avenue we think might give us a lead.'

'We'll keep on it, Neil,' Kim said.

'There *is* one more thing,' McGovern said to his daughter. 'Miles is up here to stay.'

'Really? That's good.'

'Yes,' Tate said. 'I had put in for a transfer and it was granted. Then I had a call from my boss and he said Neil here needed some help, so I did my magic before leaving London. Well, I say *I* did, but my team were doing all the hard work of course.' He smiled at Kim.

'We bosses have to delegate, son,' McGovern said. 'Welcome to Edinburgh. Are your things on the way?'

'They are indeed. I got a new place in Learmonth Gardens. I bought it sight unseen, but the cleaners have been in giving it a good seeing-to.'

'We'll need to have a party,' Kim said, smiling.

'We will indeed.'

She raised a glass. 'Here's to Miles coming to work for us.'

'To Miles.'

They chatted for a while, had some more wine and then left the restaurant, stepping into the biting cold.

'Boy, it certainly is colder up here,' Tate said as McGovern's driver pulled into the side of the road.

'I'll see you in my office in the morning,' McGovern said.

'Yes, sir.'

They shook hands.

'You too, Kim.'

'Goodnight, Dad.' She kissed her father on the cheek and he got into the Range Rover.

'He's a good guy,' Tate said as McGovern was driven away.

'He is.'

'You want me to see you into a taxi?' Tate said. 'I'm staying at the Radisson and there's a taxi rank over there.'

Kim nodded to the flats that overlooked the High Street and the corner of Cockburn Street. 'I live there. The entrance is on North Bridge.'

'Great. You got time for a nightcap in the bar across the road?'

'I'm married,' she said, smiling.

'I know you are. To Frank. Neil told me. But no offence, it really was just meant to be a nightcap in the hotel bar, no further. But maybe some other time?' He smiled at her.

'Some other time.' She watched him cross the road and thought, *Another place, another time.*

TWENTY

Harry felt tired when he got up, a combination of stress, long hours and maybe a wee Glayva before bed. The three women in his life – his daughter Grace, still a toddler; his wife Alex, back from the dead; and his sister-in-law Jessica, the woman who had been his rock for almost a year – were up and about, doing what people normally did at breakfast time. Kettle on, toaster trying to burn bread without setting the kitchen on fire, the wee machine that ripped the insides out of an orange to produce a thimble's worth of juice.

Life going on, whether he liked it or not, or even wanted to be a part of it. He did. But this morning something was in his head with Doc Martens on, giving him a kicking from the inside. And to make matters worse, the girls were listening to a radio station he hated that played music that wouldn't have seen the light of day twenty years ago. He wondered how some male rappers felt when their core fan base was ten-year-old lassies. He shook his head, then winced. *Stupid bastard.*

'You look like you haven't been to bed,' Alex said.

'I haven't. I slept down here last night, before showering and getting dressed again.'

Jessica was feeding Grace before getting ready to take her to the nursery he owned.

'You'll burn yourself out, Harry,' she said.

'You will,' Alex confirmed.

'It's this damn crossbow case. They were being protected by the government, yet somebody found out who they had been in a different life and killed them. Not the father of their victim. He's got an alibi for the estimated time of death.'

'We checked Smith out in Fife,' Alex said, 'and there were no arrest reports or anything. No red flags.'

'There wouldn't be. His name was flagged in Neil McGovern's system. That's why he and Kim turned up at the crime scene. They wanted to know what was going on with him.'

'I'm assuming Neil talked to Smith's handler?'

'Of course. They're investigating everybody who was in the chain to see if they can find a leak. Maybe one of them got fed up with some scumbag getting preferential treatment and decided that a more suitable punishment should be meted out.'

'We need to find out who discovered the true identities,' Alex said. 'And did they kill the pair or pass the information along? It's frustrating. I have a feeling that Neil McGovern himself will be going above and beyond.'

'It doesn't seem fair,' Jessica said. 'That poor girl was shot in the head by that pair and they're the ones who got all the taxpayers' money thrown at them.'

'What would you have had done to them?' Harry asked her.

She smiled, but there was no humour there. 'Put it this way: if they'd done that to this little lamb, I would have wanted them thrown to the wolves.'

'And that was clearly somebody else's viewpoint,' Harry said, taking a slice of blackened bread out of the toaster. 'Do the wee dials on this thing not work or something? This looks like it's been damped down by the fire brigade.'

'Scrape it over the sink,' Alex suggested. 'It actually tastes better that way.'

'Compared to what? Eating the embers out of a campfire?'

He scraped it with a butter knife anyway, but left the edges still dark as it turned out to be too much like hard work. Butter on, he sat at the coffee table after making a cup of instant. Strong and black.

Harry's phone rang. He picked it up after washing down a piece of toast that tasted like it had been pulled out of a litter bin.

'Hello?'

'Harry, it's Stewart. You out your pit yet?'

'I'm having breakfast.'

'That doesn't really answer my question, son, but I'll assume you've got your kegs on. Listen, we got to talk to a witness last night. He got the plate number of a stranger seen leaving the victim's stair. The car belonged to Craig Smith.'

'Our victim through here?'

'The very same. Either he drove through here and killed her and then shot himself in the head with the crossbow, which is very unlikely, or somebody shot him first and then took his car through here and shot his accomplice.'

'Maybe he could have shot himself through the head, then somebody went into that caravan and took the crossbow but didn't report the crime.'

'Aye, maybe. We can't rule that out, but I would put that thought on a back burner. I would think that Smith was killed and then the killer took his car through here to Glasgow and killed his girlfriend, knowing if somebody spotted the car and took the plate number – which somebody did – then it would lead to another dead end. We need to find that car. Meantime, I'm going to ask McGovern what the result was when he spoke to the families of the victims. They're in protection too, so I'm sure he's had a word with them.'

'There's a "be on the lookout" out for the car. We might get a hit from that.'

'Go and check out where Smith worked. He was fired from the financial place after the assault and then he got a job in a furniture warehouse. No doubt with McGovern sponsoring him.'

'I hope they kept him away from the hammers,' Harry said.

'He should have been bloody well locked up.'

'We're still working on it. Maybe he was leading a double life that McGovern didn't know about.'

'Right, Harry, son. I have a wee job on today: DCI Mike Holland. I spoke to his wife and she said he's coming back down from his mother's place in Golspie.

I told her to call him and get his arse into Helen Street or else I'll have the bastard suspended.'

'Keep us in the loop, sir.'

'Count on it.'

TWENTY-ONE

Mike Holland drove his car like he was having his first flying lesson. Booting the bollocks off the car, he bypassed Inverness and kept on going, only stopping for a piss and a stretch of his legs at Pitlochry. Touching sixty brought with it aches and pains in places he never knew existed. His days of running after scallies had been left behind a long time ago. His wife had suggested they take up running after he retired, but he put that down to a momentary mental breakdown. The limit to his physical movements would be to take the dog out for a pee.

The A9 was fraught with danger at every turn as usual, with arseholes in German pocket rockets and big SUVs that could climb a mountain but were only used for picking up kids from school.

He made it into Fife and it felt like coming home, just like it always did. Glasgow was his real home, but he always got a strange feeling here, like he belonged here. Maybe it was something in his genes or whatever; he couldn't explain it. For years, before he had met his mother, whenever he had gone to Burntisland with the girls in summer, he'd felt like this was home. Maybe it was a tribal thing; his family were here and maybe there was some kind of subconscious pull.

Now he was back in Fife, he had the feeling again. He drove along to Kirkcaldy and parked at the side of the art gallery. His brother, Walter, was waiting in his own car. He got out when he saw Holland pulling in.

'Walter! Good to see you again!' Holland hugged the older man, who stepped back and looked at him.

Holland looked around to see if Hugh was getting out of a car, but no other door opened.

'How you keeping? How's your mother?' Walter asked.

Holland blew his breath out. 'My mother passed away a couple of days ago.'

'Good God, I'm sorry to hear that. Come on, let's get in out of this cold and we'll have a coffee.'

They walked into the entrance and went to the café, where they ordered a coffee and sat at a table.

'What happened to Helen?' Walter asked.

Holland took a sip of the strong coffee before looking at his brother. 'She had cancer and didn't tell me.'

'Was she in hospital?'

'In Golspie. I got there maybe half an hour too late. If I had known, I would have gone there much sooner. But she died with a priest in the room.'

'Small blessings. At least she didn't die alone.'

Holland nodded. 'How's Hugh?'

Walter shook his head. 'Wee bastard. He'll get there eventually, but it took a lot out of him meeting you that one time. He has to get his head round it all. I told him we were meeting up, like I always do, and he usually answers me, but he didn't this time. I haven't heard from him in weeks.'

'I'm sorry to hear that.'

'Don't be. It's how we roll. Hugh's always been a bit quiet. Don't take it personally.'

'I don't, trust me.' More coffee. 'I met a friend of my mother's. A lady. She was nice. But I found out that my uncle had been up there and had taken some stuff. He said it was my mother's wishes that he take it and keep it for me. He's an oily wee bastard, though.'

'Is the funeral going to be up in Golspie?'

Holland shook his head. 'No, it's going to be in Dunfermline. She wanted to be brought home.'

'I thought her home was up in the Highlands, you said?'

'She said that when she left, but the priest said she wanted to be brought down here. He's a nice bloke. I got to know him a fair bit. He was standing in for another priest in Brora, but he works here in Glenrothes. He's officiating.'

'I'd like to come along.'

'That's fine, Walter. I mean, you knew her when she was pregnant with me. That's a long time.'

'I knew her then, but I hadn't seen her in a long time. My dad spoke of her after I found out he was having an affair with her.'

'I found a journal that she had started about ten years ago. I had said to her once before, why don't you write about your life? I kept bugging her and she finally did. Not that she told me, but it was there for me to read. I think she wrote it knowing I wouldn't read it until after she was gone.' Holland debated whether to tell his brother about the things that were in the journal, the part where Helen thought their father was a serial killer.

'Did she mention what happened to her career in the police?'

Holland sat in silence for a moment, wondering where this was going. 'What part?'

'How she resigned after being disciplined?'

Holland stared at his brother for a second. 'She never wrote about that. What happened?'

Walter drank some more coffee. It was warm in the gallery. He unzipped his jacket before carrying on. 'Look, Mike, this is not a slight on your mother. Okay? This is just what my dad – our dad – told me. We were having a pint one night. He was investigating a series of murders. Women found in parks. The uniformed patrol would get a shout and they'd go and check things out, and if a senior officer was needed at the scene, they'd get called in. Just like now, I assume. Well, Phil said that when he got to each scene, Helen and her patrol partner were there, but on two occasions he got there quickly to find Helen interfering with the crime scene.'

'Interfering? In what way?'

'Touching the corpse. He asked her what she was doing, and she said she was looking for clues. He told her she was contaminating the scene. He reported her. He had finished with her, but he said she was very persuasive. He started up the affair again. But he was a real ladies' man. He had been having an affair with another WPC, and she ended up being a victim. Thank God my dad had an alibi for the estimated time of death for the woman. He was shocked by the killing. It really tore him up. I think he found solace in Helen's company.'

'Did you know our dad and Helen had another child?'

The look on Walter's face told Holland that he did not. 'Another child? When?'

'Almost five years after I was born. He died. She refused to go to Edinburgh again, and somehow she ended up in St Andrews giving birth. The baby was transferred to Dundee, where he died.'

'Jesus. I thought Phil had stopped seeing her to be honest. He never mentioned her again after a while, and nobody saw her around. He did tell me one time, though, that he had bumped into her. She was no longer a police officer. She had resigned.'

'Fired? What did she do?' Holland knew in his heart what his brother was going to tell him.

'Interfering with a crime scene again. She said she wanted to get into CID, but back then, in the sixties, it was nigh on impossible. She argued that she could do a better job than half of the lazy bastards they had in CID. That was enough for the bosses, so they booted her out the door.'

'Christ, she never wrote that in her journal. That little nugget was kept secret. All those years, she told me she had been in the police, then transferred to the MOD police at Rosyth naval base.'

'That part, no doubt, is true. Pardon me for being blunt here, but I think Helen used the truth very sparingly.'

'She hated our dad. She had nothing good to say about him.'

Walter nodded. 'She wouldn't, because she acted like a spoiled child who didn't get her own way. But if our father was so bad, why did she carry on seeing him? Why did she have another child with him? Listen, I went into the house one day and she was sitting there. My mother was away visiting some member of her family, and as soon as she was gone, Helen was round at the house. This was around Christmas, nineteen sixty-seven.'

'Christ, she'd have been pregnant then.'

'Pregnant and sitting having a drink. She was sitting by the fire in my living room, her back to me and my girlfriend. Now my wife. She remembers that too.'

'I don't think Helen ever gave up the idea of being with our dad. She was ready to step into your mum's shoes at a moment's notice.'

'Dad hated that. He was a romancer, and he had a few girlfriends on the go, but he was happy to stay with his wife.'

'If you don't mind me asking, did your mother know about his girlfriends?'

Walter nodded. 'She did. She turned a blind eye, for whatever reason. I personally think that she wouldn't have made it on her own, so having him come home to her was better than having nobody coming home.'

Holland's phone rang. It was a number he didn't recognise. He answered it anyway. 'This better be good,' he said. 'I haven't finished my coffee, so you've got thirty seconds.'

'I better talk quickly then. This is Detective Superintendent Calvin Stewart, Helen Street. Get your arse over here. You have thirty minutes.'

'Oh, right. What is this about?'

'I'll tell you when you get here.'

'I'm actually on compassionate leave, and I'm nowhere near Glasgow.'

'Where are you?'

'Kirkcaldy.'

'*One hour. Or you'll be suspended.*'

'What? Suspended? What are you talking about?'

The line was dead.

'Everything okay?' Walter asked.

'Some DSup from Helen Street wants a word.'

'You have to leave?'

Holland shook his head. 'He's not my boss. I'll make a call and get it sorted. Fucking talk to me that way.'

'When's your mum's funeral?' Walter asked.

'The funeral director should let me know anytime. He's arranging it for Dunfermline crematorium. It won't be long, he said.'

'I suppose your uncle and auntie will be there?'

'Aye. Uncle Dick. We have a mutual hatred of each other.'

'Don't lower yourself to his level, Mike.'

'It's hard, Walter.'

Walter looked down into his coffee mug before looking at his younger brother. 'I've been wanting to talk to you about something else my dad said, but it's very sensitive.'

'You can tell me anything. I'm sure my mother only painted a picture of what she wanted me to know.'

The older man nodded his head, and waited until a young woman had walked past. 'My dad was talking in the pub one night. We were having a drink like we sometimes did, and he was getting wired into the whisky. This was after he told me he had split with Helen for good. I don't know if he was spinning me a line or not, but he talked about Helen and why he thought she was forced to resign from the force.' Walter took a deep breath and blew it out slowly.

'What was his opinion?' Holland asked.

'He thought Helen had stolen earrings from the victims. The women who were killed and left in the bushes in the parks. He was forever the detective. You'll be like him, I suppose. Always asking, "What if?" I was never a copper, as you know, but he would always talk shop. Then this one night, he was three sheets to the wind, and I practically had to carry him home. And you know what he said?'

Holland shook his head.

'He said, "I think Helen killed Sharon." Sharon was one of the young women our dad had gone out with. This was at a time when he'd had yet another falling-out with your mother. He'd started dating Sharon on the side. Sharon was a WPC.'

'Why would he think Helen had killed her?'

'I asked him that, and he said he had bought

Sharon a nice pair of diamond earrings and she wore them all the time. She had called him the night she died, telling him she wanted to meet up after she had been out with her friends. Phil told her he was working a case and they were all in the incident room; said he'd see her some other time. Later on, he and his team got a callout about a woman found murdered in a park. It was Sharon. Helen was the uniform on duty who was called to the scene, just like she had been called to the scenes when the others were found. She and her partner were always first on the scene. When Phil got there, he noticed the earrings were missing.

'It was years later, he said, when they had rekindled their romance, that he noticed Helen was wearing earrings just like Sharon had worn. He asked her where she'd got them and she said they had been her grandmother's and she'd left them to Helen.'

'And Phil couldn't prove anything?' Holland said.

'No. They looked like the pair, but he couldn't tell for sure. He didn't question her further, but he always suspected that she was a killer. She was working for the MOD police by that time.'

'Did he try and have a look in her jewellery box or something?' Holland asked.

'He did. They were round at a little flat she had by then in Dunfermline. But there was no sign of any more jewellery.'

They sat in silence for a moment.

'If that's true, Walter, then my mother was a serial killer. Which is funny, because I've just read her journal and she said that Phil was a serial killer. That he had taken jewellery from victims as trophies, and he had given her a pair of opal earrings that had belonged to a victim. They were in her jewellery box in Golspie. I have them in my possession.'

'She was wrong, Mike. You see, Phil wasn't the only one to turn up at the crime scenes; he had a young sergeant with him. Every time a woman died, Phil had an alibi. His sergeant told me that. I went to talk to the sergeant, who's older than me but is still as sharp as a tack. Those murders stuck with him for a very long time afterwards. He knew Phil was going out with Sharon, but he was sure Phil wasn't her killer. There were six of them in the incident room all evening. Phil's alibi was cast iron. Same for the other murders. Phil might have been an old bastard, but he was no killer. I think your mum was trying to do a number on him. No offence.'

'None taken.' Holland thought back to the journal his mother had written. In the back of his mind, way down in a deep recess, he had given thought to why Helen was always the first one on the scene. Could she have murdered the women before she went on duty?

This was a scenario that had gone through his head. He couldn't switch off being a detective, and when he had read for the third time that she had been the first one on the scene, a red flag had gone up. Hadn't a red flag gone up in Phil Nichol's head? Or had he just ignored it? That was the most likely thing. Especially since he thought she might drag him down. Or had she somehow tried to implicate him?

Whatever the case, his mother had manipulated his father, he knew that now. Just like she had tried to manipulate Holland for all these years, telling him he shouldn't try to see his father or his brothers or it would cause so much trouble. And nothing could have been further from the truth.

'Listen, you can stay with me and Jean if you want until after the funeral. Save you booting through to Glasgow and back.'

'I appreciate that, Walter. Just text me your address.'

Walter took his phone out and sent Holland a text. 'There. Jean will be pleased you're coming over.'

Walter's phone dinged. 'Bloody wee bugger. Hugh says he can't make it out to meet you, but if you want, we can go round to his house.'

'That's fine. Let's go.'

TWENTY-TWO

Harry parked his car behind the mortuary van in Broomhouse. The sun had come out, but it did nothing to brighten his mood. Alex had started talking about summer holidays, but that was three months away. Yes, it would be nice to go to a place in the sun, but if he started seriously thinking about it just now, he'd want to go right away.

Alex was the more rational one out of the two of them. Plan ahead and then look forward to it. He was the impulsive one.

Elvis walked over to Harry's car and stood waiting on the pavement, hands in his pockets, stamping his feet like it was winter or something.

'Elvis, what have we got?' Harry said, getting out of the car and locking it. He saw there was an audience already, people looking out of their windows, some standing at their front doors, gawking at the patrol vans, the police cars and the mortuary van. The ambulance was sitting there as well, just in case a miracle was going to happen, but Harry didn't think it would be needed if what he had been told was true.

'Young man badly decomposed,' Elvis replied as they walked across to a block of flats. A small dog of indeterminate breed but with a huge pair of metaphorical balls stood and barked at them from the safe distance of its front door while looking through the legs of its female bodyguard, her curlers at the ready to be fired at any advancing detective.

'Cause of death? Something that would bring out MIT, I assume, or are they erring on the side of caution?'

'Finbar O'Toole is in there, examining the body. To be honest, he hadn't said by the time I got out of there. I almost chucked my breakfast. I had muesli, so nobody would have known the difference, but it's horrible. He's bloated and his skin has turned black. He looks like he's about to pop, and the smell is –'

Harry held up a hand. 'So we're sure he's dead then?'

'And some. A neighbour called it in after the

smell became unbearable. She said the place usually stinks of pish, but this was something way beyond that.'

They walked up the pathway leading from the street, past a uniform standing at the entrance and up the stairs to the first floor. Already Harry could smell the odour. Why had it taken so long for somebody to make a phone call?

But he knew why they hadn't called. The people round here didn't call the police. They dealt with problems on their own. One of them got hurt, they all got hurt. And then somebody had to pay.

He could imagine them huddled together speaking in hushed tones, whispering about what they should do about the smell coming from number three. Then it would be decided that somebody should make the phone call. Better to have somebody as a point of reference when the polis turned up so they didn't go hunting for the source. It would be a female, somebody who could pull off being concerned. Not sexist, just psychology. Harry had seen it before.

They would pass on any information they had before fading into the background. There would be no other witnesses, nobody who had seen or heard anything. They didn't know the man who was staying here. He kept himself to himself. They didn't see him going about much. That's what they would say. It would be well rehearsed, like they were putting on a Shakespeare play.

They walked up to the victim's flat, shoes scuffing the concrete steps. Harry took out a tub of nasal vapour rub and touched some under his nose.

'I don't suppose I could have some of that, sir? Forgot mine.'

'What? And use a finger that's been nose-picking, or arse-scratching, or God knows what else, or a combination of all of the above? Fool me once, shame on me and all that.'

He pocketed the little tub and walked past another uniform at the door to the flat.

'They're inside,' the young man said.

Harry stopped. 'What's your name, son?'

'Barry White, sir.'

Harry looked at him like the young guy was taking the piss.

'Good friends with Marvin Gaye and Ray Charles as well, are you? Maybe Bob Marley?'

'No, honestly. I get this all the time.' The uniform grinned at Harry.

'Right then, let's rewind. You see me approaching and you tell me they're inside. Is that in case I didn't see all the activity going on inside for myself?'

The smile dropped. 'Sorry, sir. I was just trying to be helpful.'

'Put it into gear before you let your tongue start flapping in future,' Harry said. The pair of Doc Martens were dancing in his head again. He walked on past and into the smell zone itself.

Frank Miller was in the living room with Finbar O'Toole. He was trying not to stare too much at the corpse.

'Fucking smell's getting to me, boss,' Miller said.

'Where's Lillian and Julie?'

'Doing the door-to-door, asking about this cretin, but they won't have much luck. You know how it is in these places. They're all deaf and blind until one of their bairns goes missing.'

The living room was furnished with comfort in mind and not in any way meant to impress a guest. The settee had wooden arms and looked like it could have been used as an implement of torture in a former life but had settled into retirement as a place to watch TV for short bursts.

The TV was old and if not exactly from the cathode-ray tube era, then it wasn't a kick in the pants off it. A coffee table in front of the settee looked like it had been rescued from the tip at Sighthill and its former owner hadn't been too bothered about discouraging his cat from using one leg as a scratching post. It obviously doubled as a dining table, judging by the remnants of Chinese food in containers on it. Chopsticks lay abandoned, like the victim had given them a go before resorting to a fork. It had maybe been chicken fried rice at one time but now looked like dead maggots.

A recliner chair sat over to one side and it had some suspicious stains, but nothing like its cousin, where the owner had spent his last few seconds in life.

There was a sideboard against one wall, looking so old it wasn't beyond the realms of possibility that it was a time traveller from the seventies and had somehow ended up in this flat and was just biding its time before hopping back.

Harry pulled on latex gloves and grabbed one of the brass handles on the sideboard and opened it. There were magazines inside, ranging in taste from cars to video games to porno. Behind door number two on the worst game show ever was a bottle of vodka and two glasses. Harry closed it and stood up straight.

'What's your best educated guess on this one, Fin?' Harry asked the pathologist.

The smaller man was on his knees on a carpet that was dark brown, negating the use of a hoover on a regular basis and helping to hide the blood that had spilled from the creature that was once a human being.

Harry clocked the face; it was indeed black and puffed up, like the chemicals and gases inside had ganged up on his insides and were threatening to break free.

'He's been dead maybe two weeks. Whoever killed him turned the heating right up. It was on full blast when we came in. It's off now, but it messed with the time of death.'

Finbar was dressed from head to toe in a protective suit, including a face mask and a protective face shield. He'd be okay if the balloon that was the deceased's face popped, but the rest of them, Harry included, would be royally fucked.

'Is there a cause of death that you can tell?'

Finbar stepped to one side and pointed to the dead man's groin. There were things there that had shrivelled up.

'Is that...?' Harry said.

'It is indeed. Somebody cut his cock and balls off

226

and left them in his lap. He definitely bled out where he sat. I can't tell yet, but I'm making an educated guess that the femoral artery was sliced as well. It's what I would do if I was going to murder somebody this way. Just to make sure. You see, just cutting off the genitals doesn't guarantee death. Not in every case. Shock might have killed him, but I don't think his killer would have left any details to chance.'

'Was there any ID on him?' Harry asked, averting his eyes now. There was no chance in hell he'd be at the mortuary for this postmortem.

'I found a wallet on the dresser over there. Driving licence says he's Donald Carlisle. From Glasgow originally, but there's mail there with his name on it that's addressed to him at this place.'

'Have you run his name through the system?' Harry asked Miller.

'I did. If this is indeed the occupant of this flat – and looking at him, he could very well be Lord Lucan – he was charged with raping a lassie. But he got off lightly with a six-month sentence.'

'Christ, I remember reading about him. Manky wee bastard. He probably came through here because everybody back home knew who he was.'

'Looks like somebody wanted revenge, just like the pair with the crossbow arrows,' Elvis said.

'I'm sure there were a lot of people who would have had a pop at him if they'd found out where he lived,' Harry said.

Just then, his phone rang. It was Calvin Stewart. He stepped out into the lobby to take it.

'Sir?'

'Harry, I got hold of DCI Mike Holland. He was the arresting officer in the case of those two kids who killed that lassie with the crossbow. And the bastard is giving me the fucking runaround. I told him to get his arse down here to Helen Street and he said he's on leave. Get up there, Harry. Jimmy Dunbar spoke to his wife, and apparently he's fucking about with his brother. I got an address in Kelty where he'll be. Go and speak to the bastard. I want him interviewed.'

'Will do, sir.'

'You'll get there before I do. Make sure the bastard doesn't leave. We'll blues and twos it. I'll kick Holland's arse. Let me know if he gives you any shite and he'll be sweeping the canteen until he retires, which is only six months from now.'

'I'll get going now, sir.'

'Do that. If you have to have him physically restrained by uniforms, do what it takes.'

Stewart hung up and Harry walked back into the living room, where the bogeyman was very much alive and kicking and sitting in a chair waiting to explode.

'I'm going over to Fife to interview one of our own,' Harry said to Miller. 'Fun times.'

'I'll keep an eye on things here.'

Harry nodded and took his eyes off the thing in the chair.

'Look after my crew, Fin. See you around. Just not at your establishment.'

'Gotcha,' Finbar said as two of his assistants came in with a thick body bag.

Harry had made it out to the stair when he heard a collective, 'Oh fuck!'

He didn't hang around to see what had happened. He just knew.

TWENTY-THREE

He walked along the corridor of the Edinburgh Royal Infirmary, the floor shiny and clean and smelling of antiseptic. It was a smell he hated, the odour permeating every pore, every surface, until you couldn't shake it off. He would hate to work in here, to have his nostrils targeted by it every day. Did the staff get used to it? Did they even notice it after a while? They probably did, and then they themselves would smell of it. They would take it home with them and then their homes would smell like the hospital, their cars, their spouses and children. It was like a plague.

He was sweating by the time he got to the café. Fucking place got on his nerves. He didn't like coming here, but sometimes he had a delivery to make. He smiled inwardly at the thought. A delivery of sorts: death.

Just the thought of delivering the final blow to some old bastard gave him such a buzz, he thought he would pass out. But he was finished now, and finally he was walking back out into the cold, fresh air.

He hated this building. It had no soul. At least the old Edinburgh Royal Infirmary had beauty, designed by architects with some imagination. This place was another big box, functional but soulless.

He hadn't been back here since he had killed Paul Hart. Gus Weaver had taken the credit, just like he knew the man would, but that was fine. He preferred to kill and stay in the background.

He had come here today to visit somebody, not to kill them but merely to visit them. But he did have some more killing to do. In fact his victim would be waiting for him. Not waiting for him as in sitting with the kettle ready to go, but he was waiting nonetheless. He just didn't know it yet.

It was stuffy in the car, so he rolled the window down to let some of the chill air in. He didn't want to be sitting sweating like a bastard.

He put the car in gear and headed out of the

hospital. He felt the excitement creeping in now, the buzz he got every time he killed somebody.

And today had been no exception.

He smiled at the thought, at the memory of the bastard's face as the life ebbed out of him.

And the next one was going to be very soon.

TWENTY-FOUR

Mike Holland had never been to this part of Fife, a wee working-class village slap bang in the middle of the Kingdom called Kelty. He'd heard his mother talk about it, of course, but he'd never had a reason to come here.

He and Walter parked their cars on the pavement next to a Fife Council van that had seen better days. It looked like the side was being held on by rust, and clearly the budget was being spent on updating their vehicles. The council had always been a favourite moan of his mother's when she lived in Dunfermline.

Holland got out of his car and waited for his brother to do the same.

'Nice street,' he commented to Walter.

'Nothing wrong with it. If you like that sort of thing.' Walter grinned.

'Which one is Hugh's?'

Walter pointed to the first block of four houses on the right. The entrances to both the lower level and upper level were on the side of the building.

'That's Hugh's door over there,' he said, pointing to the back one. 'The open one.'

They started walking along the path to the door.

'Does he always leave his door open?' Holland asked, the copper in him wanting to offer an opinion on how that wasn't the best idea these days, with scallies running about and a Crown Office who were big on giving a slap on the wrist to offenders.

They approached the open door. Inside, stairs led up to the left.

'Hugh? It's Walter and Mike. You up there?'

No reply.

'Maybe he's having a nap or something. Come on, let's go up.' Walter took the first step, but Holland put a hand on his arm.

'Let me go up first.' He took out his extendable baton.

'Whoa, what's going on?'

'No answer in somebody's house? Hope for the best, prepare for the worst.'

'Fair enough. Lead the way.'

They stomped up the stairs, making enough noise that if Hugh was maybe entertaining himself, he'd have time to shout down to them, but no shouts came. There was no noise from a TV playing, or music. It was deadly silent.

'Maybe he's sleeping,' Holland said, but then at the top of the stairs he smelled an odour he had smelled before, many times.

'Walter, stay here,' Holland said.

'What's wrong?'

'Please, just stay here.'

But Walter was having none of it. He barged past Holland and marched straight ahead to the living room. Where Hugh was sitting against the door that led into the second bedroom. Except he wasn't sitting as such; he was hanging by his neck from the door handle. His face had turned purple and his tongue was sticking out.

'Hugh!' Walter shouted at the top of his voice, rushing over to his younger brother, but Holland held him back.

'Walter! He's dead. You can't go near him.'

'Let me go!' the older man shouted, but Holland kept a firm grip.

When Walter calmed down, Holland let him go and put his baton away.

'Why did he do this?' Walter asked. 'Why would he kill himself?'

'We need to call this in. We can't touch him until the pathologist gets here.'

'Oh my God. I'll have to call his sons.'

'Don't get them round here, Walter. We can't have anybody barging in here.'

Walter walked over to a chair and sat down. 'Why, Hugh, why?'

TWENTY-FIVE

The saying 'a wing and a prayer' sprang to Harry's mind as Lillian O'Shea took the exit for Kelty at high speed. His foot was buried so far into the footwell of the pool car, he felt he could kick the windscreen washer bottle.

Of course, she brought the car's speed down like an expert, but he was a nervous passenger.

'Which way now, boss?' she asked, the siren still screaming.

Harry pointed right, wondering if the car was fitted with a defibrillator. 'Left, then right at the roundabout and follow to almost the end. There's a wee dead end, but I'm sure the other polis cars will be a dead giveaway.'

Lillian kept her speed down, and a few minutes

later they saw the ambulance, a patrol car and a black van. She parked with two wheels on the pavement.

They got out and walked along the path to the open door, where a uniform was standing. Harry and Lillian showed their ID to him before going upstairs, the smell hitting them as soon as they got to the landing.

A uniformed sergeant was standing looking down at a man who looked like he had hanged himself on a doorknob. Two other men were standing around, while a third was examining the body.

'Who are you?' the younger of the men said, marching towards Harry.

'DCI Harry McNeil, Edinburgh Division. DCI Holland?'

'Correct.'

'We finally meet.'

'What do you want here?'

'You're wanted for an interview. I'm here to escort you to the nearest station. Cowdenbeath, I believe.'

'I'm going fucking nowhere. As you can see, my brother's just died.'

'You'll do as you're fucking told!' another voice from the landing said. Calvin Stewart came thumping along the hallway, face flushed, out of breath, looking like he was about to become the second corpse in the room.

The pathologist stood up. 'We'll get him back to the mortuary in Dunfermline and do a postmortem.'

'Listen to me,' Stewart said to Holland, stepping forward. 'We're going to the station for you to be interviewed whether you like it or not.'

'Oh? And why is that?' Holland said, turning back to face the DSup.

'I have orders from DCS McKenzie in Helen Street to have you interviewed. We're taking you to...' Stewart looked to Harry for the answer.

'Cowdenbeath.'

'Cowdenbeath. If you don't come along, I'm going to place you under arrest on suspicion of murder.'

'Murder? Who am I supposed to have murdered?'

'Let's go,' Stewart said, ignoring the question.

Holland shook his head. 'Walter? This is going to be a circus very shortly with the forensics people. They'll want to interview you too. Get a solicitor. Tell them the truth and you'll be fine. I have to go with these people. Stay strong, brother.'

'Bastards,' Walter said, his face a mask of pure hatred.

Stewart ignored him.

'You want me and Lillian to drive him?' Harry said.

Stewart nodded. 'Aye, do that. I don't want to hear any more of his fucking lip.'

TWENTY-SIX

Cowdenbeath police station looked like it was maybe a shop in a past life. They took Holland through the back door, like he was a common criminal, and straight to a waiting interview room.

Inside, Harry and Calvin Stewart sat opposite Holland. It was a manky room, like it had been needing a fresh coat of paint before it had become a police station and somebody had forgotten. It smelled of stale sweat and had the air of somebody's vomit that nobody had been able to fully clear. It was hot and Harry undid his tie a bit.

'Listen,' Holland started after the recorder was running. 'I didn't mean to come off as an arsehole back there, but my mother just died and now my brother. Jesus.'

'Let's start with a clean slate then,' Stewart said. 'We want to ask you about Kevin Tulloch and Heather Thom.'

'Those two? Pair of bastards. I remember getting the call that a young lassie had been found with an arrow in her head up north, and we were sent to arrest them.' Holland shook his head. 'Then they got put into protection. They got off lightly if you ask me.'

'Somebody seems to think so,' Harry said. 'They were both found murdered. One outside Edinburgh and the other in Glasgow.'

Holland's eyes widened and it seemed to be genuine shock on his face. 'That's why you said you were going to arrest me on suspicion of murder? Well, it wasn't me. I've been up in Golspie for the past couple of days.'

'They've been dead for weeks,' Stewart said.

'Oh, shite. That's bad. But why would you think I murdered them?'

'We're just interviewing people who had access to them,' Harry said.

'I had no access to them after they went into the system when they were released from prison. That was a whole other department. I couldn't tell you what happened to them.' Holland sat back in his chair. 'Listen, I'll take a polygraph. Anything you want. If you can narrow down a time of death, I'll give you an alibi. These days, it's work and home. My wife and I are planning a holiday after I retire. I'm keeping my nose clean. I want to walk out with a full pension. Why would I throw my life away on those two reprobates?'

'No love lost on them then?' Stewart said.

'None at all. Doesn't mean I wanted to kill them. I didn't even know they lived in Glasgow after they were released.'

A look passed between Harry and Stewart. Did he genuinely not know that Craig Smith had lived in Burntisland, or was he a good actor? He would certainly know how to play the game.

'We don't know how their identities were leaked. If you were to hazard a guess as to how that happened, what would it be?' Harry asked.

Holland shrugged his shoulders. 'It would have to be within the system. Somebody found out who they were, had a hatred for them and either let their names loose on the internet or killed them themselves.' He looked between the two officers. 'Or maybe one of them gave the game away. You know how some prisoners like to brag. What if either of them boasted about what they had done and that now they were walking free?'

'It's a possibility,' Stewart said. 'We're trying to piece together their lives, like if they were members of any clubs, something like that. Somewhere they would go and then they start talking about their past lives. Or maybe just one of them did that and put both their lives in danger.'

'Listen, I swear to God I had nothing to do with those deaths. I'll help you in any way I can. Ask my wife if you narrow down a timeframe, and she can tell you if I was at work or at home.'

'Sorry to hear about your mother dying,' Harry said. He knew what the other DCI was going through, having lost his own mother just a couple of years ago.

'It was hard. I got there just too late. But a priest was there. He helped me a lot.'

'At least you weren't alone,' Stewart said. 'Spiritual guidance helps sometimes.'

'Aye, he's a good guy. He was working up there, standing in for another priest. His church is down here in Glenrothes. Father Dan O'Brian. He was a tremendous shoulder to lean on.'

'We just wanted to talk to you about this because

you were the arresting officer, DCI Holland,' Stewart said. 'Thanks for your help. You're free to go, but keep yourself available if we need some help from you.'

'Of course.' Holland stood up. 'Again, I was just stressed out. Now my brother's dead, not long after my mother. I mean, what are the odds?'

'A team from Fife will be assigned. Sorry for your loss.'

Stewart and Harry stood up and they all shook hands before Holland left. The uniform who had been standing outside closed the door behind Holland.

'What do you think?' Stewart asked.

'I can't see him being responsible. He has a clean record. Commendations. Six months away from being able to sit in the sun all day. Why would he risk it?'

'Aye, I don't think he's in the frame for it, Harry. But it bothers me that on the day he comes down from Golspie, his brother commits suicide.'

'Doesn't mean to say there's any sort of connection.'

'Right, I'm going through to Glasgow, but I'll be back in Edinburgh in a few days,' Stewart said.

'Right, sir. I'll call Alex and brief her on what went on through here today.'

'Take care, son. Catch you later.'

TWENTY-SEVEN

Walter had thought about calling his wife to let her know what had happened to his brother, but he didn't want to shock her. She didn't handle bad news too well.

He got in his car and headed out of Kelty after they had taken Hugh's body away in the mortuary van. He lived in Ballingry and had promised Mike that he would take him to meet his family one day. Though it had been a shock for them all to discover a new member of the family, they had accepted him.

He decided to stop to buy a bottle of brandy from the corner shop not far from his brother's house. Jean might need a glass or two when he broke the news. If she didn't like it, he would maybe arse it later. *Better buy some tinnies as well then,* he thought.

He parked outside the small store and nipped in, trying not to let the image of his dead brother's face jump into his mind every five seconds. He was sure he would be seeing it in his dreams later that night.

Fifteen minutes later, he was pulling into the driveway of his house, in a small street tucked away from the main road.

'Jean?' he said as he walked inside. 'I'm home.'

There was no reply.

'Jean?'

He walked into the living room, but it was empty. The kitchen was off the living room, but that too was empty.

He walked through to the bedroom and found his wife in bed. With an arrow in her forehead.

Walter sucked in a breath and held it there. He wanted to scream, to shout, to do anything, but he was frozen to the spot.

'Sorry it had to end this way,' a voice said behind him. 'But I have a question: do you want to go out like your brother or take a bottle of pills? Slit your throat maybe? That's a good way, so I've heard.'

Something snapped inside Walter, making his

heart race, and he turned round at the voice. The figure was holding a crossbow.

He was confused at first, thoughts spinning in his head, and for a moment he felt his bladder go weak, but he fought it.

'You did this to my Jean? Why?'

The man's grin was wide across his face. 'I'm your brother. When you got the email, you should have ignored it. Didn't you think it would bring you grief?' The grin was fading now.

'No, I didn't think it would bring me grief. Why would I? I knew I had a brother.'

'Phil was a filthy old bastard, fucking anything with a pulse. Including my mother. She just died, and Phil had never made peace with her. He's a disgusting old monster.'

'I can't help what my father did,' Walter said.

'*Our* father. You were an older teenager. You could have expressed an opinion.'

'My father was strict. He wouldn't have listened to me.'

'Well, he could hardly have listened to me, could he? I was brought into this world when you were an adult. You could have tried. I heard horrendous stories about him, how he would treat women like shite, just like my mother.'

'Look, I'm sorry your mum died, and she wasn't happy when she left this earth, but the past is the past. Why don't you put the crossbow down and we can talk?'

The man laughed. 'Just like on TV. I don't think so.'

'Did you kill Hugh?' Walter's voice was faltering now.

'Of course I did. I was going to give him the crossbow treatment, but he fought back. I strangled him, which they will no doubt find out when they do the postmortem on him, but by then I'll be long gone. I have to go and speak to somebody else before I disappear, but it's all in hand. One more of your scurvy bastards, then my job is done. Then I'll be so far away, they'll never be able to catch me.'

'You killed my brother. I don't believe this. Just because he was Phil's son?'

'Exactly. I could hardly kill Phil now, could I? Considering he's already in the ground. Is that where you're going, in the ground? Or are you going up in flames?'

'I want to be buried next to my father and mother.'

'Helen's being cremated. Know what I'm going to do after that? Take her ashes and scatter them on

250

your dad's grave. Then they'll be together.' The man laughed hard. 'Together forever.'

Walter knew then that his brother was insane. His legs started to shake, then the shakes gripped his whole body. He knew he was going to die. What was the alternative? Living here without Jean?

Either way he didn't have a choice.

'You want to lie down on the bed next to Jean? Or die where you stand?'

Walter let out an animal grunt and charged at his brother, but he was older and his reflexes weren't as sharp as they had once been.

His brother fired the crossbow, and at that close range the arrow entered through Walter's right eye and lodged there, stuck in his head. The momentum of the arrow wasn't enough to stop Walter, but it slowed him down slightly. His brother stepped aside and Walter fell to the floor and ended up on his side.

'It wasn't meant to end like this, but you know, say hi to Phil for me.'

TWENTY-EIGHT

Mike Holland stopped to look at the block of flats. He was in the east side of Dunfermline, and the area was halfway between pride of ownership and junkie city.

He stepped forward and climbed to the first landing. It was open to the elements with boards across the landing, designed for an aesthetic look but making the place look like it was boarded up.

He knocked on the first door. The house of horrors. More commonly known as his uncle Richard's home.

A young woman answered. His daughter Lizzie. 'What do you want?' she asked him. Her hair was long and straggly, like she had given up on brushing it a long time ago. She had a pleasant face, the kind of face some old-timer lady might call bonnie.

'I'd like to speak to your dad, Lizzie.'

'I don't think he wants to speak to you.'

'Please.'

She turned away from him for a second and shouted, 'Hey, Dad! That Holland bloke is here.'

Holland rolled his eyes. Charming.

'What does he want?' they heard Richard reply.

Lizzie looked at Holland. 'What do you want?'

'I heard him. Tell him I'd just like to talk to him for five minutes.'

'He wants to talk to you for five minutes.'

'Och, fuck me.' Silence for a moment. 'Five minutes, that's it!'

'Five minutes, that's it.'

'I'm not deaf, Lizzie,' Holland said as she stood back to let him in. He walked forward into the lobby and waited for the thin woman to shut the front door behind them.

'He's in the living room,' she said, which didn't help him.

He held his hands open. 'I've never been here before.'

Lizzie tutted and gently nudged a door and it

swung open. 'The living room. I'll give you a grand tour of the mansion later on if you want.'

'I look forward to it. Meantime, maybe a cup of tea.'

'Aye, that sounds like a good idea, Lizzie, love,' Richard shouted from inside.

Lizzie tutted and scuttled away, while Holland went into the room.

Richard was sitting in a recliner chair. Holland could see a walking stick standing on its own steam next to the chair.

'So, you've come down to give me a belting then?' Richard said. 'I'd expect nothing less from you.'

'We both said harsh things, Richard, I admit, but I just wanted to have a wee talk with you. Without us getting into some sort of pagger.'

Richard looked at Holland. 'You're making the place untidy. Take a seat.'

They could hear Lizzie bashing about in the kitchen with the kettle, and opening a couple of cupboard doors and shutting them again as if she had forgotten where the chocolate Hobnobs were kept.

The living room was better kept than Holland had imagined it would be. The furniture looked reasonably well kept, but the flowers on the cream fabric wouldn't have been Holland's first choice. There was a flat-screen TV in one corner on a stand that held a DVD player and another black box. There was a china cabinet behind the door and Holland stared at the contents for a second.

'The bus isn't there. The toy one you mentioned. The one that sat in Helen's cabinet. She showed it to me one time, ages ago. I don't know why you thought I would have taken it. Bloody accusing me of going up there and nicking stuff? Christ, I know you're a copper, son, but you were way off bat there.'

Holland noticed for the first time that Richard's trousers were pyjama bottoms. Richard pulled them up to show a bandage round his knee.

'I'll be getting this off soon. I had to have a knee replacement. I've already been off my feet for three weeks.'

Holland stared at the bandage, his heart sinking. He knew then that Richard hadn't been up to Golspie.

Richard pulled the trouser leg back down. 'I haven't been over the door in weeks.'

'Sorry, Uncle Richard. I really mean that.'

'Aye, well, you can't just go about accusing people of doing shite. You're not Nazis.'

'I didn't realise you had problems with your knees.'

'Milk and sugar?' Lizzie shouted through.

Richard nodded to Holland. 'She's asking you. She already knows what I take.'

'Just milk. Please,' Holland shouted back.

He knew that maybe, just maybe, Richard could have had help in getting into a car and Lizzie could have driven him up to Golspie.

'She doesn't drive,' Richard said, as if reading his thoughts.

'What?'

'Lizzie. She doesn't drive. Never wanted to. She never married, never had kids, holds a steady job, but she gets the bus everywhere. Or a taxi when she goes out on a ladies' night out. I could see the wheels turning in your head.'

'My adoptive dad had to have a knee replacement. The cartilage wore away.'

'Oh, I wish that had been the problem.'

Lizzie came in with two mugs, a packet of Jammie Dodgers under her arm. Holland hoped they hadn't been opened yet and was pleased to see they were new when she put them down on the coffee table in front of him.

'Thanks, Lizzie.'

She made a non-committal grunt as she left the room. Holland picked up the packet of biscuits and waved them at Richard. 'You want one?'

He turned up his nose. 'Like I'm not already a fat bastard. I mean, I'm not exactly a horse, but I've not been able to move much, and I put on weight just looking at a packet of biscuits.'

'So, what was wrong with your knee, if you don't mind me asking?'

Richard looked at him. 'I was shot.'

The Jammie Dodger had only made it halfway on its journey to Holland's mouth before it was rudely interrupted.

'What do you mean, you were shot?'

'Some bastard broke in to rob us, and we surprised him. Or Lizzie did, anyway. I was sitting here watching TV and Lizzie had been out with her pals and she forgot to lock the front door. And you know how some of those wankers are: they try door handles and sometimes they come up lucky. His luck was in that night. He came in to rob the place and he was carrying a crossbow. Who does that? Go on the rob and carry a fucking crossbow? I mean, it wasn't a Robin Hood thing, it was one of those new, folding things. You can hide one under your jacket, they're that small. Lizzie screamed at him, then he took aim at me instead of running. But Lizzie had some of the hooligan juice in her and she ran up the lobby and shoved him. The arrow went into my knee instead of my chest.'

'What did CID do?'

'Came round and wanted to me to look at a photo book, but I told them it was dark; he was nothing more than a shadow. Even Lizzie hit him in the dark, and she'd been drinking. I'm still waiting for an update.'

'Christ, Richard, I want to tell you something: that was no housebreaker. You were targeted. Have you got anywhere else to stay?'

'Naw, just here. I'm not running away from some arsehole.'

'If he comes back, you're a dead man. He's already killed people with a crossbow.'

Richard leaned over to one side of his chair and lifted what appeared to be a machine gun. But it wasn't. It was a crossbow.

'Jesus. It was you.'

Richard smiled. 'Away ye go, ya daftie. I bought this fucker online after that bastard came in here and shot me. Here, take a look at it, but mind it's loaded with five arrows that are in a magazine on top.'

Holland saw the arms of the crossbow hadn't

been extended out and he carefully took it from Richard. 'I've never seen one like this. How does it work?'

'The arrows have a shield. You take it off, load them into the top, then pull the ring holder out. Extend the arms and you're ready to fire. Then you sort of break the thing in the middle like you would a six-shooter and that loads the next arrow. He had one with him. That's what he shot me with, but he didn't have time to reload before Lizzie shoved him and started screaming. He ran off.'

Holland shook his head. 'That's how he could easily walk about with a crossbow without raising eyebrows. He could shove it under his jacket. Bastard.' He looked at his uncle and handed the crossbow back. 'They thought I killed two people with a crossbow.'

'Where were they killed?'

'Glasgow and Edinburgh. I arrested them twelve years ago as teenagers. They had killed a girl with a crossbow in a caravan.'

'Christ, I remember that story from the papers! They were put into some kind of protection after that.'

'They were. And now somebody's found out who they were and killed them.'

'How would somebody find that out? Don't they spend millions protecting bastards like that?'

'They do. It's a complete failure of the system when somebody is in protection and they end up murdered.'

'They must have bragged, that's my opinion. One of them spoke out of turn. Maybe got pished in the pub and blabbed it out.'

'Maybe.' Holland ate a biscuit almost automatically as his mind went elsewhere, then he washed it down with some tea.

'Listen, Richard, I want to ask you something else, and bear in mind, she was my mother as well as your sister, so I'm not slagging her off.'

'Okay. I'll keep an open mind.'

'Years ago, I asked Helen to write a journal. Talk about how she had me and how she met Phil Nichol. Just so that if I had questions in the future and she wasn't around anymore, I'd have the journal.'

Richard looked puzzled. 'Your mother actually wrote something? I would believe that when I saw it. Helen never wrote anything in her life. She barely got through her homework.'

Holland reached into a pocket and brought out the journal he had found in Helen's car. He passed it over.

Richard looked at it. 'First of all, when she joined the polis, I was the one who filled in the application form for her. Her writing could best be described as a chicken pissing in snow. It was awful. She said she was going to practise hard so if she got in, her writing would be better for filling out a report. She did improve, but she always printed. It was legible, but she would have won no awards for penmanship skills.' He opened the journal and flipped through the pages without really reading any of it, before passing it back.

'Sorry to tell you this, Mike, but that's not her handwriting.'

'How do you know?'

'When she moved up to Golspie, she wrote me a wee note telling me what things were like. She used email of course, but she was always about sending people cards. As long as she didn't have to write long stuff in them. This is not her handwriting, I can assure you.'

'Who the bloody hell wrote it then?' Holland said.

'No idea.'

'In it, she talked about how she thought Phil Nichol was a serial killer. How he had nabbed some earrings off some victims. Dead ones. But my brother

Walter said she was asked to resign because she had interfered with a crime scene.'

Richard laughed. 'Interfered with a crime scene? Let's tell it how it was, Mike: your mother was a thief. She got caught stealing from a corpse. Not by Phil but by her partner. He dropped her in it because he was scared he would get caught up in it all. They gave her a choice: resign or get fired. The polis didn't want the bad publicity and the lawsuits, and she didn't want to be fired and ruin any chance of a new job. She told them she had sold the earrings. She couldn't help herself. She told me she wanted to shove it right up them.'

Holland risked another Jammie Dodger and again washed it down with some tea. 'Look, I know now that you were laid up with your knee, but one of Helen's friends said she saw you coming out of the house. And there's a laptop missing as well as the wee bus.'

'She's mistaken, Mike. It wasn't me, obviously. Why would she think it was me?'

'It was somebody who had access to her house.'

'What about a neighbour? There was some rum bastard who'd just got out of the jail. Young guy. I can't remember his name. I think Helen mentioned him a few times. She thought it was unusual, him getting that house, because all the others were occupied by people who had retired.'

'When was this?'

Richard looked at him. 'A while back. A few years ago. He might have come back or something, I don't know. Golspie isn't exactly a hot spot for crime.'

'His name wasn't Craig, was it?'

Richard snapped his fingers. 'That was it! Do you know him? Has he got form?'

'No, I was just thinking about somebody. But this man was seen maybe a week or so ago.'

'That nosey old bastard next door to her, he's a real charmer. It wouldn't surprise me if it was him.'

'Do you remember her having a laptop?' Holland asked.

'Aye. She kept a shitey old one with nothing on it, but she had a newer one that she did all her emails and stuff on. She reckoned if her house got tanned, they might find the old one that she left out in the open and think there was nothing else.'

Holland thought that this was exactly what had happened. Somebody came into her house and took the old laptop, not realising that there was another one. But why take the model bus? There was some significance there. He didn't know what just yet, but it was there.

'Do you know how long Craig lived near Helen?'

'Just a few months. He was a bloody menace. To be honest, she reported him to the housing authority, and a few days later, he was gone. She couldn't believe it.'

'That must have been between times when I visited her.'

'Aye probably. As I said, he wasn't there long.'

Holland drank more tea. 'Listen, again I'm sorry about shouting on the phone. Helen had just died –'

Richard held up a hand. 'No need for apologies, son. I said some stupid things. I think I was just lashing out and said some horrible things. Truth is, Helen was so excited when you came back into her life. Especially since I was away living in London. I only came back up here a few years ago, as you know. I wish I'd never gone down there.'

'We could spend all our lives wishing we had made better choices.' Holland moved his arse on the settee. It wasn't the best and he couldn't imagine sleeping on it, and if the chair was the brethren of the settee, Richard must have been in a lot more pain than he was letting on. Unless he had strong meds. If so, maybe Holland would ask his uncle for one before he left.

'Did you know Helen had another son and he died?'

'Oh aye. She was the talk of the toon. That was why she went away. She was still in the polis at that time. But then the wee guy died and she went back to work and then she got caught. She went to work in the MOD polis. It didn't stop her seeing Phil, though. He was a soft bastard. By God, he loved the women. She bumped into him one day, and they started things up again. She worked on the gate at Rosyth and it was shift work, but they managed to see each other. He was still married.'

'She didn't tell me that. I thought she got married to some guy she met in a bar?'

'That was later on, in the late seventies. It didn't last that long. I don't think he got along with her son.'

'What do you mean? I never met the guy.'

'Not you. The other one. She had another baby with Phil Nichol. But she kept this one.'

'I never knew that. She never told me,' Holland said.

'He was born in nineteen seventy-three. You met her, when was it again?'

'Nineteen eighty-nine,' Holland said. 'I was twenty-six. And a detective.'

'He'd have been sixteen. She could easily have hidden him from you. He could have went and stayed with his pals or something when you visited. I mean, did you ever just drop in on her unannounced?'

Holland shook his head. 'No, never. I always called first.'

'There you go then. I'm sure she wanted to see you, but she never wanted you to meet your brother. She had another son and she kept it a secret from you. You've got to ask yourself why she would keep her other son from meeting the one who was in the polis.'

Holland stood up. 'I need to make a call, Richard.'

TWENTY-NINE

'You don't seem so nervous as a passenger today,' Lillian O'Shea said to Stewart.

'You can see that bloody big tractor in front of you, can't you? And we're doing what, fifteen miles an hour?'

'Ten,' Harry said from the front passenger seat.

'If Old McDonald there would get a fucking move on, maybe we could have a word with Walter and still get back down the road for tea.'

'I'm sure he doesn't like driving along these country roads with frustrated drivers behind him,' Harry said.

Lillian cleared her throat and gave Harry a look.

'Frustrated passengers, I mean,' he corrected himself.

'Thank you,' she said with a tone.

The big John Deere indicated right and then turned into a field.

'Thank fuck for that. And let's learn a wee lesson from that, shall we, Miss O'Shea,' Stewart said. 'When the nasty man in the back of the car says, turn right, he means right, not left and then right after you find out you're going the wrong way.'

'Lesson learned, sir.'

'Good. But look on the bright side: I've always wanted to come on a tour of Lochgelly.'

'Glad I didn't disappoint.'

'Right, Lily, right. Head for the A92.'

She booted it down the road and indicated left for the motorway slip road.

'Ignore the wee sign pointing right for Auchtertool,' Stewart said.

'I've got my Apple Maps on, sir.'

'Didn't fucking help when we left the station, did it? Maybe you should have put it on before we left there.'

'She's doing fine, Calvin,' Harry said.

'It's my job to berate the lower ranks, Harry. Lily and I are just fine.' Stewart patted Lillian on the shoulder.

Harry was looking at his phone. 'Walter still isn't answering his phone.'

'Maybe he took offence when we said we wanted to have a quiet chat with him,' Stewart said.

'Or he could have contacted Holland and given him a heads-up and Holland told him not to talk to us.'

'It was always going to be a toss-up, Harry. But the daft old bastard gave us his address. If we stay on this motorway, then get off somewhere up the road in Glenrothes, it looks like it isn't too far from there.'

'Christ, it sounds like a monkey wrote those directions. No wonder Lillian here is confused.'

'That's bad patter, Harry, son, trying to blame this all on me.' Stewart sat back and couldn't help but look over his right shoulder as Lillian joined the traffic.

'See? I managed to do that without getting us creamed by a tipper.'

Stewart tutted. 'Bloody show-off. You're worse than Robbie Evans.' He nudged her playfully on the shoulder. 'Did you hear about young Hamish O'Connor falling out of a tree with his fucking skids round his ankles? He could have blown the whole fucking undercover job he was on.'

'And you broke his balls over it,' Harry said.

'Not yet, but give me time.'

Twenty minutes later they took the Bankhead Roundabout and followed Apple Maps until they found Walter's house in the middle of a housing estate.

'There's his car,' Harry said. 'I saw it parked outside his brother's house.'

Then Harry's phone rang. It wasn't a number he recognised, but he answered it anyway. 'Hello?'

'Harry? It's Mike Holland. Where are you right now?'

Harry debated whether or not to tell the man he was at his brother's house, but then just went with it. 'We're at Walter's house. We need to get a statement from him about what he saw in Hugh's house.'

'No, you're not. You're there to ask him about me, but that's fine. I would be doing the same. But listen, I just found out something: my mother, Helen, had another son. We need to talk.'

'We can meet up after we've spoken to your brother. Give us a little bit of time. Where are you right now?'

Holland said he would text Harry his uncle's address. *'The poor old bastard was shot in the knee with a crossbow. I think he came here to kill him for some reason.'*

'*Less of the old,*' Harry heard a voice say in the background.

'Jesus. But we're here now. Let me go and I'll call you back shortly.'

Lillian stopped the car behind Walter's and they got out into the chill air. There was a hint of fog waiting to come down and blanket everything.

'Holland's uncle was attacked in his house,' Harry said. 'Shot with a crossbow, but he survived.'

'Christ Almighty,' Stewart said. 'He was lucky. We'll have to call the locals and see what they have on that case.'

They walked up to Walter's door and saw it was ajar. Harry knocked and gently pushed the door.

'Walter? It's Harry McNeil and DSup Stewart. Can we come in?'

Then Harry smelled it, the last thing he'd been expecting to smell when he came here.

'Gloves on, batons out,' he said to the others, and they went inside.

THIRTY

The smell was rank, but nothing they hadn't smelled before. Each of them stood looking down at the remains of Walter Nichol. Blood seeped from his head wound into the beige carpet. The smell was almost overpowering as it invaded the house.

'Obviously, he's not been dead long,' Harry said. 'Since we just saw him a little while ago.'

'The bastard must have been waiting for him,' Stewart said. 'Let's check the place out in case he's still here.'

They stepped over the body. Harry looked into the kitchen, making sure nobody was there. It was empty. He followed the other two out of the living room and into the back hall. The bathroom was on the left, while two more doors were further down.

Stewart turned the handle on the first one and eased the door open. It had a single bed and was sparsely furnished. He stepped in and opened the wardrobe door. Nothing.

Lillian opened the other door and found Jean's body, half sitting up with the arrow in her head.

'Jesus. Collateral damage,' Lillian said.

'He must have come here to kill Walter and found Jean here,' Harry said. 'He killed her to silence her and waited for the old boy.'

'We need to call this in,' Stewart said. 'I'll do it. Harry, you call Holland. You better get him to get his arse over here, but don't let him come inside. Lillian, knock on a couple of doors, see if they saw anything.'

Harry nodded and left the house, stepping back outside into the cold air, Lillian right behind him.

'Why would he kill the old couple?' she asked Harry.

'I think it's got something to do with what Holland said about him having a brother. His mother had another son they didn't know about. Remember, Walter knew about Holland but Hugh didn't. They just met Holland a while back. Somebody wants the secret kept maybe, for whatever reason.'

'How do we find him, though?'

'He's hiding in plain sight. Bastard. Now, go and

see if anybody saw anything while we wait on the uniforms and everybody else.'

She walked away to the next-door neighbour's house and Harry called Holland's number. 'Mike? It's Harry McNeil. Change of plan. You need to come to Walter's.'

'Why? What's wrong? Is he alright?'

'Just come as quickly as you can.'

THIRTY-ONE

Half an hour was all it took to turn the small street into a funfair. Neighbours came out to see what all the fuss was about, and that made the uniforms' job that much harder, trying to identify who stayed where, who saw what and where they were when they saw something.

Mike Holland stood by his car, hands shoved deep into his pockets, shivering.

'I can't fucking believe this,' he kept saying. 'I only saw him this afternoon. How could he have been murdered in the short time since I saw him?'

'It happens,' Harry said. 'And you said you have a brother you didn't know about. Which means you have a full brother, if your mother was telling the truth to her brother. And if he's telling the truth.'

'He has no reason to lie.' Holland gave a bitter laugh. 'You would think she would have told me, especially since he lived with her.'

'And you never saw him at all?' Stewart said.

'Not once. Not fucking one time. He was a teenager by the time I met her. Sixteen. Old enough to go to a friend's house every time he knew I was coming over. I can't believe she was such a sneaky old cow.' Holland looked at his two colleagues. 'I thought I knew her, but then I find out what a manipulative bitch she was. And obviously he is too. I showed my uncle the journal my mother had supposedly written, and he said that wasn't Helen's handwriting.'

'And you didn't get a chance to talk to your mother at all when you went up there?' Stewart said.

Holland shook his head. 'I left a message on her answering machine telling her I was coming. She was already in the hospital, so she wouldn't have got it.'

'And she died just a short while before you got there?' Harry asked.

'She did.'

'I would say there are no such things as coincidences, but we know your mother had cancer,' Stewart said. 'But that still begs the question:

where was your brother when all this was going down?'

'I have no idea,' Holland replied.

'Did he live up there with her?' Harry said. 'And maybe just kept out of your way when he knew you were coming?'

'He might have done. I mean, I have literally never met the man. But that reminds me: a young man got out of prison and was put into one of the pensioners' houses in Golspie. His name was Craig. It could have been Craig Smith, aka Kevin Tulloch, your crossbow victim. The man you thought I'd murdered.'

'We were just doing our job,' Stewart said.

'Aye, I know. But what if my other brother met him too? What if he didn't like Helen getting too close to him? My mother would help anybody, so she would probably have taken Craig under her wing.' Holland stared off into space for a few seconds before looking at Harry. 'My mother's neighbour said she saw somebody coming out of the house with some stuff. She thought it was my uncle, but it couldn't have been. He's recuperating from knee surgery. What if it was my brother? The one I didn't know about?'

'How will we know?' Harry said.

'Your guess is as good as mine. But somebody was in her house creeping about.'

'Was anything taken?' Stewart asked.

'A model bus, and an old laptop that was a decoy in case her house got tanned. She had a new one...' Holland looked at the others. 'I have it. In my car.'

'Go get it then, pal,' Stewart said. 'No, wait, we'll come with you. My bollocks are about to fucking fall off.'

They walked across to Holland's car, and after he got the laptop bag from the boot, they sat inside, Harry in the back. Holland was in the front passenger seat and he booted the HP up.

'My mother left a note for me that the password she used for everything was the place I first met her and the year. Hillend, nineteen eighty-nine.'

He typed it in and they all looked at the machine like it would suddenly burst into song, but it merely whizzed its fans and Holland navigated to the photos folder.

'You think she would have put photos of your brother on here?' Harry asked.

'Don't you keep photos of your kids?' Holland said. 'If you have any, that is.'

'I have two. And yes, I do.'

Holland opened the folder and scrolled through

the photos. Like most people, Helen had filled it with photos that were only interesting to her. Then he saw her standing next to a young boy in Blackpool. On the beach. In front of the Pleasure Beach amusement park. Then more scrolling through the years.

'She's got a lot,' Harry said.

Then more recent photos. Of Helen, with her friends. In the pub. At a wedding. Then Holland hit pay dirt, the photo jumping out at him like a fist.

She was standing next to him, Holland's secret brother, under a banner that said 'Happy Birthday' and then his name.

'Christ. That's him. He's a bit younger there, but there's no mistaking him.' Holland explained where he had seen the man before.

Harry looked at Stewart. 'There's nothing concrete, you realise that?'

'Of course I do; I'm not fucking daft. If we jump all over the bastard, he'll walk. Fuck.'

Holland's phone rang. He looked at the screen. 'Sorry, I need to take this. It's the funeral director.'

Stewart took the laptop and continued scrolling through photos while Holland spoke. After a few minutes, he hung up.

'My mother's funeral is two days from now.'

Harry nodded. 'That'll give us time to get the team on board.'

'Agreed,' Stewart said. 'Two days, then maybe we can nail the bastard. But I think we're only going to get one chance at this. Then he's in the wind. Now your mother's gone, Mike, he will be too.'

THIRTY-TWO

'I'm going to have dinner with Miles and my dad tonight,' Kim Miller said to her husband. 'You don't mind, do you?'

'Mind? Why would I mind my wife having dinner with Superman Miles?'

'Oh, come on, Frank. It's just dinner with a colleague.'

'Yeah, well, we all know how it starts out.'

'For God's sake, you're not jealous, are you?'

He was silent for a moment before shaking his head. 'Nope. Sorry. It's been a long day.'

They were in a conference room along from the incident room in Fettes. Kim was sitting at the head of the table, swinging her chair from side to side.

'Are you sure everything's alright? You've been acting funny lately.'

'I'm fine, Kim. I just wish you would find some time for us now and again. We have the kids, we have our work, but sometimes we just need you and me time, like the old days.'

She sat forward in her seat and looked at her husband across the table. 'I'm sorry if I haven't been giving you attention lately. Work has been a bitch.'

'Tell me about it.' Miller drummed his fingers on the table like he was trying to beat the shine off it.

'Listen, Craig Smith, your victim, was sent up to Golspie, out of the way, after he kept getting into trouble. He was told he would be there permanently if he didn't behave himself. He made friends with an older woman, Helen Wardlaw. She's the mother of DCI Mike Holland. Smith was there for a month, then he asked to be moved to somewhere more exciting. So they moved him to Burntisland.'

'Great, thanks for that.' Miller seemed to stare off into space for a moment.

Kim smiled at him. 'I'll make it up to you soon, I promise. In fact, we could lock the door and maybe we could put this table to better use.'

Miller grinned. 'Really?'

'No, of course not.' She laughed at him.

'I'm glad you think our sex life is funny,' he said. 'Maybe Miles will put you in the mood.'

Anger suddenly crossed her face. 'What, like you and Carol?'

'What are you talking about?' Miller asked her.

'Liken when you go and put a wreath on her grave at Christmas.'

He held his hands open, making a face.

'I was getting your suit ready for dry cleaning when I found a receipt in one of the pockets from Waitrose for winter flowers. You didn't give them to me, and unless you have a girlfriend, I figured you had put them on Carol's grave. Tell me I'm wrong.'

'You're not wrong. It was only flowers. I didn't see the harm.'

'Putting flowers on your dead wife's grave. Some people would see that as you not being able to let go, even though you're happily married. You *are* happily married, aren't you, Frank?'

He didn't answer her question. Instead, he suddenly stood up and walked out of the room.

'Frank, listen, we can talk about this,' Kim said and walked over to the door. But he was going through a door further down the corridor.

'Shit.' She closed the door behind her and started walking along towards the incident room. She had been ignoring her husband recently, and she couldn't blame him for being pissed off with her, but she was in line for a promotion and was working extra hard. So what if he had put flowers on Carol's grave? She probably would have put them on Eric's grave if he'd died. It would blow over. She hoped.

Miller called Harry McNeil and had a word with him about Craig Smith. Then he hung up and left the station and got in his car. Kim had a fucking cheek chastising him about taking flowers to Carol. Once again, his thoughts were of Alex McNeil coming back from the dead. Everybody had thought she was dead, including Harry, and all the people she worked with, but she had been in protective custody for nearly a year because of a threat to her family.

Harry was reunited with her, and although Miller was pleased, he wished his own wife had been in custody instead of a coffin.

He had got on with Carol far better than he got on with Kim. Yes, his wife was funny and sexy and had a will of her own, but Carol had been like that too and she'd really known how to make him feel loved. Kim was concentrating on her career just now, and he was glad for her, but maybe having a baby with him hadn't been the best choice. He loved his daughter Annie, and his stepdaughter Emma, but they were always at a babysitter's, Emma after school and Annie all day. He didn't feel Kim was bonding with the baby as much. He had wanted her to cut back a little, spend more time with the kids, but there was always some kind of meeting to go to. And now she was having dinner with her father and this Miles guy.

Fuck.

He drove round to the Waitrose store and went into the flower section, where he bought a bunch of flowers and a bottle of *The Famous Grouse*. Then he drove up to the cemetery, letting the receipt go out of the car window. For spite, he thought about leaving it in his trouser pocket again, but no, this was his moment.

He parked in Warriston Cemetery. He hadn't been here in three months, since just before last Christmas. It had been cold then, the coldest December in twelve years. It was cold now, but he didn't feel it.

He got out of the car and walked across to Carol's grave, the flowers in one hand and the bottle in the other. He stopped at the headstone and read her name. And that of his unborn son, Harry.

He put the flowers down and stood up.

'God, I wish you were here. You remember the good times we had, the laughs we had? I miss those days like you wouldn't believe.' He smiled at the cold stone. 'Maybe one day soon I'll join you and young Harry there. You never know.'

He felt a thump in his chest, a heavy weight dropping like a stone. He cracked the seal on the whisky and took a few gulps of it, smacking his lips.

'*Hey.*'

The voice sounded like wind rippling through the trees at first but then he heard a footfall behind him, just a shoe crushing some grass. He spun his head and his breath jammed in his throat and he couldn't breathe for a moment.

'Carol?' The woman standing behind him was dressed in black jeans and a black coat. Her blonde hair was just as he remembered it. Her smile was just as beautiful, her eyes shining like two orbs of glass.

'*What's all this talk?*' She took a few steps towards him, and he fully turned to face her.

'How?' He shook his head like he didn't fully understand and didn't want to. 'I was just thinking out loud.'

'*I miss you, Frank. You know that don't you?*'

'I miss you, too. I wish you hadn't died. Oh God, I wish you hadn't died. I miss you so much.'

'*Aren't you cold? Come on, let's sit in the car.*'

She reached out a hand and he held back for a second, not because he felt fear, but because he felt something far deeper than that. He felt the love come back into him, like some kind of heat. He put the top back on the bottle then reached out and grabbed a hold of her hand. It felt warm. He'd expected it to feel cold, like his did, but it was warm and soft. She waited until they were side by side, and he walked her round to the passenger side, opened the door for her and waited until she was settled before closing the door.

He walked round the front of the car. It was dark and the interior light went off. He couldn't see her inside, and he didn't think she would be there when he opened the driver's door. But she was. She smiled across at him.

'I can't believe you're here,' he said to her, starting the car. He didn't want to go anywhere; he just wanted the heat.

'*This is nice,*' she said.

'It is.' He took the cap off the bottle again and took a swig, feeling the liquid burn as it went down his throat. 'Want some?' He held the bottle out for her.

She shook her head. He took another small swallow. He could smell her perfume now, the one she always wore when they were going on a night out.

'*Won't your wife be expecting you home?*' she asked him, her smile still in place.

The question shocked him for a moment, like she shouldn't know he was married again, that Kim was in his life. He was here with her, Carol, and couldn't care less that Kim knew or might find out. But the fact that Carol knew about Kim bothered him. Made him feel guilty.

He made a noise and tried a smile but failed. 'No,' he said, his voice feeling dry. He took some more whisky. 'I couldn't care less, to be honest. That's why I'm down here with you. Sitting in a dark cemetery, drinking whisky, with my wife.'

The words came out easily, and it felt so natural. He knew he was standing on the precipice now, but it felt good, felt better than anything he had felt since the day of the funeral, years before.

Carol gave a soft laugh, and he saw her eyes glistening in the dark, like they were filling with tears. '*I never stopped being your wife, did I?*'

'Not once. I've never stopped loving you. My

first and only true love. I wish you were next to me in bed every night.' More whisky.

'*I wish that too.*' She smiled at him and pressed the button that brought her map reading light on. She brought out a red lipstick and flipped the visor down, sliding the mirror cover along and reapplied her lipstick. When she was done she flipped the visor back up and switched the little light off.

'*You know what I was thinking about the other day?*'

He shook his head. 'No. Tell me.' His guts were warm now, a combination of the drink and seeing his wife again.

'*I was thinking about our first Christmas together in the flat in Comely Bank.*'

'I don't have that flat now. I sold it to Harry McNeil. He rents it out. I couldn't keep that place after...you know.'

'*I died?*'

He couldn't say it, not now. He drank more whisky instead.

'After I was on my own. I just couldn't do it.'

Carol reached over and put one of her hands on his. '*I understand. I really do. You don't have to blame anybody, especially yourself.*'

He almost flinched when her hand touched his,

but he relaxed and smiled, before she gently removed it again.

He drank again, deeper this time. Maybe the whisky coursing through him made his dead wife stay with him. If he stopped drinking then maybe she would just disappear.

'You were saying about Christmas?' he said, feeling his lips wet, feeling spittle flying. He wiped his mouth with the back of his hand. He wouldn't have normally done this in front of his wife, but Carol was dead, and she was also sitting in the front of his car. What if he hadn't bought the whisky? Would she have still appeared? He didn't want to think about that.

'It was the first Christmas in our flat. You had moved in with me and we had joined CID and every-thing was going so smoothly, until...'

He nodded. 'I remember.' He drank some more of the whisky and let his head rest against the headrest.

'It was Christmas Eve and we were nearly done for the day...'

THIRTY-THREE

Christmas Eve, back then

It had snowed that morning, just enough to panic the motorists and cause massive tailbacks. It slowly improved throughout the day until the afternoon clouded over and a blizzard ensued.

'You would think they've never seen snow before,' DS Andy Watt said, coming into the incident room and shaking the snow off the top of his head.

'I thought you had suddenly gone grey,' Miller said to him.

'Listen, son, I have a good head of hair and it's all my own. Salt and pepper they call this colour.

Unlike old wiggy over there,' he said, nodding to DCI Paddy Gibb, who was standing over by a whiteboard.

'I heard that, cheeky bastard,' Gibb said.

Carol Davidson laughed. Everybody was in good spirits, especially her. This was the first Christmas she would be waking up next to her boyfriend, Frank Miller, and she thought that this was the best Christmas present she could have.

The day was winding to a close when the phone rang. Carol answered and then held the receiver out for Gibb. 'It's for you, sir,' she said.

Gibb walked over and took the phone from her. 'Hello?' he said, his gruff Irish accent cutting through. Miller watched the older detective's face change before handing the receiver back to Carol.

He stood looking at Miller.

'What's wrong, sir?' Carol asked.

'There's a hostage situation in an off licence off Frederick Street.'

'Shouldn't they be calling in the negotiator?' Miller asked.

'They have. Marksmen are outside and the nego-tiator has been talking to him for half an hour. Or trying to, anyway, but the man says he will only speak to one man.' He looked Miller in the eyes. 'You.'

———

It was snowing heavier now. Rose Street Lane had been blocked off, crowds of people were being kept away from the scene. Miller was sitting in the back of a mobile incident box van, shirtless, while the tech wired him up for sound.

'Put your shirt back on,' Paddy Gibb said, sitting along from Miller. 'You're giving me the boak.'

'Jealousy will get you nowhere, sir.'

'Aye, that's what it is. Anybody mind if I smoke?'

The tech gave him side eye.

'God. I'm dying here, son. Give an old man a break, won't you?'

'I'm not telling you what you can and can't do,' the young man answered.

'It's that beady eye of yours. I light up, and next thing you know, I'm in front of the man upstairs. You know, not *the* man, of course, but the man who will put me on suspension. Not like in the old days, when everybody smoked. I take it you don't smoke, son?'

The tech nodded. 'I do actually.'

'You want to light up while Frankie boy there gets his shirt on?'

'Sure.' The tech took the offered cigarette from Gibb's packet and they huddled together while they lit up. Soon, the inside of the van looked like it was on fire.

'I hope I live long enough to actually get in that shop,' Miller said, coughing.

'Aye, right enough, he's got a shotgun. But I don't think he'll kill that lassie. If he called for you specifically, you know he's got a beef with you. He wants you inside there. Just you.'

The back door of the van opened and Lloyd Masters, head of the firearms unit, stepped in and closed the door on the invading snow.

'Jesus, I thought the van was on fire,' he said.

'Frank here doesn't smoke, so we're having a fag for him,' Gibb explained, as the tech hid his cigarette behind his back. 'Smoke it, son. Nobody's bothered.'

The tech shrugged and puffed quickly on the cigarette before nipping it and putting it in his pocket.

'This is a Glock 9mm,' Masters explained. 'The first girl he let go said he had a sawn off shotgun. To be honest, if he has you close to him, and he pulls the trigger, then there's not much chance of him missing.

If you think it's life or death, make the first one count.'

Miller nodded as he accepted the gun, checked it over, and put it in the back of his waistband. 'I just passed the firearms training, but we didn't practise pulling a gun from the back of our trousers.'

'First time for everything,' Masters said, slapping him on the shoulder.

'I just need to get the earpiece in, sir,' the tech said to Miller. 'That way you'll have audio as well as output.'

Miller nodded and the man stepped forward. He played around with the earpiece, making sure it was a tight fit, and they practised talking and listening until Miller was ready to go.

'That's you, sir,' the tech said. There were several seats at consoles, and he took one. 'I'll be monitoring you from here, and your voice will be heard through the speakers so Commander Masters will be able to hear you.'

'Great.'

The door opened again and Miller's girlfriend, Carol, stepped in. 'I'd like to be in here, if you don't mind?' she asked Gibb.

'Fine, aye, just take a seat and don't touch anything.' He turned to Miller. 'Get your jacket on

and I'll call the tosser in there and make sure he
knows you're coming in.'

'What if he wants to search me?'

Masters looked at him. 'If he's that close, there's
a pretty good chance he won't be able to point the
shotgun at you. Let the bastard have it at that point.
He might ask you to lift your shirt, but our intel says
he's on the edge and not thinking straight. It's a
fifty-fifty chance he will. If he does, you're going to
have to try and draw your gun as you pretend to
take your jacket off. You're going to have to wing it,
but the Superintendent has given you a green light.
The lassie he let go, well, he smacked her in the
face with the shotgun, breaking her nose. He said
he's going to kill the next one unless you get in
there.'

Miller nodded, and put on the waist length
jacket, winked at Carol and stepped out into the
snow.

It was a short walk along Rose Street in the show
to the off licence. Gibb said he would call the guy,
and Miller hoped the nutcase had picked up.
Marksmen were on either side of the shop, waiting to
storm the place if things went south, Gibb had said.
Which meant they would be bringing in buckets to
scoop him off the floor. He opened the door to the

shop, the bell dinging somewhere in the back to announce his arrival.

There was nobody there, not that he was expecting anybody to be up top. He had been told to walk through the door to the back and there was a door to the basement. If the shooter was planning on killing them, then that was the only way out. Unless he was planning on putting the gun under his chin.

Miller walked through, stomping his feet a little, giving warning that he was coming down.

'Darren! It's DC Miller. I'm coming down!' Darren Boyle, aged twenty-nine, labourer, lived in Wester Hailes. Just an ordinary bloke, until he had decided to take a shotgun into an off licence and make a call for Miller to visit him.

Miller clomped down the old, wooden stairs to the basement. The walls were a dark yellow, maybe stained over the years, if a load of people had stood in the stairway smoking.

At least it was lit. It turned to the left further down and Miller followed it until he was in the basement, which was stacked with the type of goods you'd expect to find in an off-license; boxes of booze.

A ginger-haired girl suddenly popped her head up from behind a row of boxes, like she had built a fort.

'I'm...Marina.'

'Hi Marina. I'm here to talk to Darren.'

'I'm here, you fucking tosser and I have a shotgun pressed to this tart's back. Tell him, Marina.'

The girl just nodded, which was an exaggeration of the shaking she was doing.

'Miller, step to one side and let the girl go past you. If you grab her and try to run, you'll never make it to the stairs.'

Suddenly, Marina was out from behind the boxes. She started running as Miller stepped aside.

'The girl's coming up,' Miller said.

Boyle stood up from behind the boxes, and Miller stopped breathing for a second. Boyle had unzipped his jacket and Miller could see the man was wearing a suicide vest, holding a plunger.

'Did you expect anything less from somebody who was in the army bomb squad? The shotgun was just for show.'

Miller nodded, getting his breathing under control. 'Why don't we just have a chat about this? You don't have to detonate that bomb vest.'

'That's it, talk through your microphone to those upstairs. I don't care. It's you and that old bastard I want. I told them on the phone. I want the two of you in here.'

'Who's the other one?' Miller was puzzled. Nobody had told him two of them were to come down here.

Then he heard the footsteps on the stairs and turned round as another man appeared. Terry Anderson. The man who had trained Miller when he was starting out in uniform.

'Terry?'

Anderson nodded. 'I'm sorry I got you into this, son.'

'I thought you were retired?' Miller asked.

'I am. They asked me to come in. I said no, but then I got a call saying Boyle wanted you down here. This is not your fight.'

Miller looked puzzled then Boyle moved forward. 'Shut the fuck up! This isn't a reunion. You pair of bastards are going to pay for what you did to me.'

'It was a mistake, son,' Anderson said.

'What's this all about?' Miller said

'Don't play the innocent, Miller. You were there right with him when he was giving me a kicking round the corner in Rose Street Lane. That Saturday afternoon after we'd been to the match in Easter Road. I was drunk, needed a piss and this old tosser followed me round. When he caught me, he beat the shite out of me.'

'I know,' Miller said, remembering that Saturday afternoon just a couple of years ago.

'You know? Yes you did. You stood and watched.'

'That's not true,' Anderson said, taking a step forward.

'Of course it is!' Boyle shouted.

'No, it's not. It's true I got wired into you, but I'm old school. Miller here came along and stopped me. He had to make a report. Him and the others who helped stop me. I was disciplined, forced into retirement and shortly afterwards, I was diagnosed with cancer. I don't have long.' Anderson pointed to Miller. 'If anything, you should be thanking that man. He saved your life. You don't remember, but you punched me in the bollocks. I saw red and got wired into you. Miller and the others stopped me. You got this all wrong.'

Boyle lowered his hand for a second, and Anderson saw his chance. He threw himself on the younger man.

'Run Frank, get the hell out of here.'

Miller sprinted for the stairs, knowing he would only have seconds to live if he stayed. If there was any time in his life when he would describe himself as flying up stairs, this was it. He moved with a stealth he didn't know he possessed as he moved towards the front door of the shop. He made it outside just as the explosion rocked the building.

He fell onto the snow as the place shook like an earthquake had just hit. Chaos ensued as people were running all over the place. Then he looked up and saw the one face he wanted to see more than anything.

'Carol,' he said, and reached out a shaking hand.

Now

The heat from the car was kicking in now, making him feel comfortable.

'That was a good Christmas,' he said, his words slurring now.

'*It was,*' Carol said. 'You were alive. I had felt so scared when you went in there. Paddy Gibb tore a strip off the team when he found out that nobody had noted that Darren Boyle was an ex-soldier.'

Miller nodded in the darkness of the car. 'Anderson had cancer. He knew what he was doing that day; he knew he was going to die and his family would still get the insurance money.'

'*He redeemed himself.*'

'I wish I could turn back the clock,' Miller said, his words barely stringing together to make a sentence. He looked at the whisky bottle. Almost empty. 'This dulls the pain, but not enough,' he said, and looked at her once more, waiting for her to disappear, but she didn't.

'*The police are coming. You might want to turn off the engine and slide over into this seat,*' Carol said. Then she opened the door and got out. She leaned her head back in as the cold invaded. '*Take care, Frank.*'

'I don't care anymore, Carol. I want to be with you all the time.'

'*You can't. Not yet. I have to go. I can't be here when the police turn up.*'

Miller reached a hand. 'Don't go, please. I love you.'

'I love you too.' Carol shut the door. Miller let the whisky bottle go onto the passenger seat and fumbled about in the dark until he found the handle to open the door and he leaned on it, falling out onto the dirt drive.

He struggled to his feet and then found a gravestone, hanging on for dear life as he vomited behind it.

He stumbled back to the car, shutting the driver's door.

'Carol,' he said, walking round to the passenger side. She wasn't there. He opened the passenger door, his head spinning now, his legs not getting the message from his brain. Nobody there.

Then headlights split the darkness, blinding him. He put up one hand to shield his eyes but the lights got brighter.

The car stopped behind his and two men got out and walked towards him.

'Evening, sir,' the older one said. 'What have we got going on here then?'

Miller pulled out his warrant card. The voices from the two men seemed more distant.

'Carol,' he said, then suddenly the gravel was rushing up to his face.

Then there was nothing.

THIRTY-FOUR

The next morning, Miller thought he had died, which wasn't a bad thing. He'd be with Carol. Despite not remembering much of what happened after the car pulled up, he remembered being with his wife.

She's not your wife anymore, a voice in his head reminded him.

He looked around the room. There was light behind the curtains, but they weren't familiar. He needed to pee so he flung the covers off, which only made his headache worse. He lay still for a couple of minutes, his bladder and his head competing for attention.

He got up slowly, and realised he was standing in his vest and skids. This wasn't his bedroom. Was this

his father's place? He stumbled across to the curtains and pulled one a little bit apart. He winced at the light even though it was dull outside.

Nope, this definitely wasn't his father's place. There was a tenement building across the way, but not Cockburn Street, which he would have seen if he'd been at his father's flat.

Where the hell was he then?

He walked across to the bedroom door, zigzagging around an invisible obstacle course and gently turned the handle. What time was it? He looked down at a bare wrist where his watch normally lived. What if he'd been rolled and they had dumped him somewhere? No, they would have left him fully clothed, lying in the gutter.

He heard noises coming from somewhere. A TV. He headed towards the sound, along a hallway. The door facing him was ajar so he gently pushed it.

'Morning, sir,' DS Lillian O'Shea said. She was fully clothed, sipping from a mug as she sat on the settee sipping a coffee. 'How you feeling?'

'Need to pee.'

'Turn back, second door on your left. If you want to shower, there are fresh towels in the bathroom. And a spare toothbrush, unopened in a packet.'

He nodded and did just that. Stripping off, he

stood under the steady stream of prickly water until he felt he was more human than zombie. He had no choice but to put his shorts and vest back on after drying off. When he went back into the bedroom, his shirt was hanging on a coat hanger, his suit on a chair that sat in the corner. His socks were tucked into his shoes.

His wallet and warrant card were in his pockets, his watch lying on top of his trousers. If the boss had been expecting him in on time, then he was now disappointed.

After he got dressed, he walked back to the living room. A mug of coffee was on the coffee table in front of the couch.

'No sugar,' Lillian said.

He nodded, and sat down, noticing for the first time, the two painkillers sitting next to the mug. He swallowed them and put the mug back down.

Then he turned to look at Lillian and said one word: 'How?'

She picked up the remote and silenced the newscaster.

'I got a call last night from an old friend of mine in uniform. He said there was a DI Miller in a car in Warriston cemetery. Or rather, puking all over it. Then the DI collapsed, drunk, on the driveway. Did

I know a DI Miller? I said I did. My friend brought you here. They helped you up the stairs, took most of your clothes off and put you in the recovery position so you wouldn't choke on your own vomit.'

'That was nice of them.'

'It was actually. They could have taken you to the cells.'

'My car?'

'Parked downstairs. One of them drove it back here.'

Miller took more coffee. 'Jesus. I think I arsed a whole bottle of whisky.'

'By the way they said you were puking, I think you might have too.'

'You know the guy, you say?'

Lillian nodded. 'He's a sergeant. We went through Tulliallan together. He's a good guy. Same with his partner who was with him.'

'Christ, I feel like I'm still drunk.'

'You look like it too. That's why I called and spoke to Harry McNeil. I told him you were feeling under the weather, you were here with me and you wouldn't be in today. I'll go in later.'

'He didn't ask why I was here?'

Lillian shook her head. 'No. Harry's a good guy. If you want to explain to him later, then fine. If not, he won't question you. You've known him for a long time.'

Miller drank some more coffee. 'Did the patrol crew say anything about the woman who was there with me last night?'

Lillian looked at him. 'No. They said it was only you.'

Miller nodded and stared at the muted TV. Of course Carol wasn't there. She was just there for him to see.

He knew he would be facing flak when he got home, but that wasn't something that bothered him.

THIRTY-FIVE

Next day

'I fucking hate places like this,' Calvin Stewart said from the passenger seat of the pool car. They'd had to park in the lower car park with all the other mourners, which didn't amount to much.

'I don't think Holland's mother was too popular,' Harry said. 'I mean, there's about ten cars here, and five are polis.'

'I told Charlie to come along and he could stab some bastard with that fucking manky knitting needle he has, but his leg is giving him what for. I told him to man the phones instead, whining bastard.'

They got out of the cars with the other mourners and started heading into the chapel. The hearse wouldn't be that much longer. Holland had called Harry and said they were leaving the funeral parlour where Helen had lain the night before, after coming down from Golspie.

'When I was through in Glasgow yesterday,' Stewart said as they walked into the chapel, 'O'Connor said to me that when the wind blows the trees in a cemetery, that's the ghosts waving them. I don't know how much more pish I can take off him. Thank Christ I'll be back in Edinburgh soon.'

'Davie Ross get away alright then?'

'Aye. He and Joan are going away soon. I think he wants to ask her to marry him.'

'Good for him.'

'I'm surprised he can still get it up, to be honest.'

'Fuck's sake,' Harry said.

'This is fucking barry. It's roasting in here. Every time I come into a warm place after being out in the cold, I fall asleep. If you hear me snore, give me a dunt.'

'Aye, watch me. No offence, but I'll be filming it and putting it on Facebook.'

'Nice to know who your friends are.'

Lillian O'Shea was behind, with Elvis and Frank Miller.

They sat down and watched as Mike Holland came in with his family, which consisted of his aunt and uncle, the latter being pushed in a wheelchair, and a scattering of nieces and their husbands and offspring. One of them was wearing a polka-dot dress under a faux fur, something that looked like she had just shot it that morning, and by the look of her, eaten it after skinning it.

More people came in, men in suits and overcoats, looking like they were going to audition for a new series of *The Sopranos*.

Father Dan O'Brian walked in ahead of the coffin. It was put on rollers and curtains were drawn over it.

The priest gave the eulogy, praising Helen for all the good work she had done with her volunteering, and saying that she was a good friend to her neighbours and all those she knew in the church.

They sang a couple of hymns, Harry having a quick look at Stewart, wondering if he was in pain given the sounds he was making, or whether he had learned a new language that consisted of whistling, wheezing and farting noises.

Then he looked over at Mike Holland's brother. The one he hadn't known about.

And the man made eye contact with him.

And then they made their way out of the church.

THIRTY-SIX

Mike Holland stood in line with his family members and shook the hands of the mourners as they left the chapel, including Miller, Stewart and the others in the team.

They headed back to their cars and Harry saw a police van parked just outside the entrance to the crematorium.

'The other mourners must think the family are a bunch of miserable bastards, not having a wee do afterwards,' Stewart said.

'It would hardly be appropriate.' Harry nudged Stewart. 'Here's Mike now.'

'I appreciate everything you've done,' Holland said, shaking their hands.

'No problem, pal,' Stewart said. 'Are you sure you're ready for this? To put the cuffs on your own brother?'

'After knowing he killed my brothers when he didn't even know them? I'm ready to boot him in the bollocks, never mind cuff him.'

'Then let's go. We'll be close by. He's not going anywhere.'

Holland walked across the car park, and Stewart and Harry followed, keeping a little way behind. Father Dan O'Brian was putting his cassock in his car and slipping on an overcoat. He looked up from the boot and smiled at Holland.

'I hope the service met with your approval?' he said, smiling.

'It was actually very good, Father. Helen would have been so proud. Especially since the service was carried out by her own son.'

O'Brian's smile faltered for a moment. Then he quickly reached into the car, swiped his cassock aside and grabbed the crossbow. 'How did you figure it out, Mike?'

'Our mother's new laptop had photos on it. She was scared of you, Dan. She wanted to make sure that if one day anything happened to her, people would know. But I think you knew that. That's why you wanted the laptop, but you grabbed the wrong one.'

'Yes, that was a bit of a blunder.' O'Brian looked around and saw the other detectives waiting.

'It's too late, Father!' Harry shouted. 'You're not going anywhere.'

'I know that. It's not going to end how you would like it to.'

O'Brian lifted the crossbow higher, but it was a move Holland was expecting and he grabbed the small weapon and pulled O'Brian close, turning sideways and sticking a leg out, tripping the priest.

Then they were all over him, Harry and Stewart running up to him – Stewart not exactly running, but making a motion that was just a hair quicker than walking. Arms and legs were flailing, and Stewart saw an opportunity when a gap presented itself and kicked the priest in the bollocks.

'God, I overbalanced there!' he shouted.

When they had him on his feet, Stewart looked O'Brian in the eyes. 'Feeling a bit chilly? Well, we've got a nice warm interview room waiting at the Dunfermline nick for you.' He nodded to the uniforms. 'Take the bastard away.'

'That's blasphemy,' O'Brian said, struggling to breathe after the kick in the chuckies.

'Is it? How does *wanker* grab you then?'

THIRTY-SEVEN

Mike Holland knew he wouldn't be able to go in and interview O'Brian, but he was content to watch the interview on a monitor.

A uniform stood guard at the door while Harry and Stewart sat opposite the priest.

'You know, I did begin to wonder if you really were a priest,' Stewart said after the tapes were rolling.

'Of course I am. Did you know Helen had even considered becoming a church minister but she thought she wouldn't make a very good one. Considering all the bad shite she had done in her life.' O'Brian smiled. 'That would have been ironic. All the bad stuff she did. All the men she fucked. She couldn't keep her knickers on, and she made a right arse of Phil Nichol. He was my father too, Mike. Did you know that?' He looked at the mirror. 'But she decided to keep me. The second bastard died, and she kept me.'

'Why don't you have her last name?' Harry asked.

'Because she married that dick and changed her name to Wardlaw. She wanted me to keep my surname.'

'Why wasn't your last name Nichol?' Stewart said.

'He wouldn't let her use it. I mean, there was nothing stopping her from using it anyway, but he went with her to register the birth and she told me none of us had his name. He was happy to sleep with her, but he didn't want the fruits of his labour having his name. Helen got divorced from Wardlaw when I was twelve, but she kept his name. Silly cow.'

'Before we go on, I want to ask you once again if you want a solicitor present,' Harry said.

'Of course not. Useless tossers. Ask away.'

Both detectives had never had it so easy in an interview room.

'Since you're in such a talkative mood, why don't you tell us how you managed to avoid Mike Holland all these years? What was it, thirty-three years?' Stewart said.

O'Brian took a deep breath through his nose and blew it out slowly through his mouth. 'Aye, it was really easy. You have to understand how sneaky my mother – our mother – really was. She was a manipulative bitch, and when she couldn't have Phil Nichol, that hardened her. Her words, not mine.

'So there we were just tooling along, getting through life, when all of a sudden she gets a letter from the adoption agency. Her son, who she had given up for adoption when he was six weeks old, suddenly wanted to come back into her life. Now, she could have written back and said no, and that would have been the end of it. Bear in mind, Holland contacted the agency, and they wrote to her without giving him her details. She had put her name on a list years before, saying she would like to be contacted if her son wanted to get in touch. So she was delighted.

'I wasn't. I told her I didn't want to meet him. She said that was fine, I didn't have to. I was sixteen and lived my own life. Helen was a shite mother. She liked the booze and the smoking and I was just there. So I hung out with friends and stayed away when he came to see her. She told him to always call when he was coming over. He never just turned up. Except a couple of times when he was coming over to Fife with his family.'

O'Brian laughed. 'Christ, one of those times, he turned up and I hopped the fence and he came round the side of the fence. She was quick on her feet, I'll give her that. She introduced me as a friend of her neighbour's. That was when she lived in the mobile home.'

'Then you joined the priesthood,' Harry said.

'No. I dodged about for two years, then I went to university in Edinburgh. Then the priesthood. I never saw Holland again. Of course I got the stories about him, how he was working his way up the ladder in the police. How super-duper a crime fighter he was. Made me sick.

'That's when I had my first kill in Glasgow. Some skanky fucker who couldn't keep a needle out of her arm. She came to me for confession. I hated being in Glasgow, but I was gaining experience. After this pond life came to see me, I knew everything about her, so it was easy to take her life. Which I did. I dumped her in Holland's area. Her murder was never solved. So much for Holland being Supercop.'

'How many more were there?' Stewart asked.

'Plenty. I would like to say I was cleaning their

souls, but that would be lying. I enjoyed it. Some-times I would get called into a hospital to give the last rites. It was easy for me to walk about unnoticed in a hospital. I could walk right past a police officer guarding a door.' O'Brian laughed. 'It was so easy. Like when I killed Paul Hart. You, McNeil, thought it was Gus Weaver, and the bastard took the credit, but I was the one responsible.'

'Let's get onto Craig Smith. Tell us about him,' Stewart said.

'Little bastard. They sent him to Golspie to teach him a lesson. He was getting into trouble and remem-ber, the government was spending a lot of money on him, protecting his identity. They put him in an empty house near my mother. She liked him of course. I thought he was a little prick. Then he told me he was going to be on his best behaviour so he could be transferred to Burntisland. I told him to come to Glenrothes where I was now working. He could come to me anytime, I said, and I'd take his confession. Bear in mind, I just saw him as a little thug who was on probation at the time. I didn't know he was in protection. That little nugget got revealed when he came to confession in my church in Glenrothes.

'He actually bragged about it, under the guise of

confessing his sins. I could tell he had enjoyed what he had done. I asked him about it and he told me about Amanda Brown. Told me their real names too. I knew I had to take him out. Take them both out. I asked him where Amanda stayed, so I could find out the nearest church for her to go for confession, and the little tool told me. And where he lived too. He was very talkative. So I killed him at home, took his car, drove down to Glasgow and killed her too.'

Harry gritted his teeth for a moment, watching this man in front of him, a man of the cloth, talking about killing people like they were nothing. He knew he had to stay professional at this point.

'Anybody else you want to tell us about?'

'You already know about him: Donald Carlisle. He was a friend of Craig Smith's. They met sometime when Smith was arrested for something. Then I read about him in the papers. Filthy bastard, raping a little girl. I found out where he lived and taught him a lesson. He pissed himself in fright, the little fucker.'

Harry made eye contact with O'Brian. 'I can't believe you're really a priest. No priest would ever talk like you do.'

'Blame Helen for that! She's the one who pushed me into this. I wanted to be a copper, just like her other son, but she said, no, I couldn't be like our old man. But Mike turned out fine, didn't he?'

'Are you responsible for shooting his uncle Richard with a crossbow?' Stewart said.

'You know I am. I wanted to get rid of the bastard. He didn't come up to visit my mother when she moved to Golspie. No, I should say, when she abandoned me and moved to Golspie a few years ago.'

'You were angry with her,' Harry said. 'We get that.'

'I was. Her whole life was a lie. Then she got cancer, and I asked for a temporary transfer because Father McLean had taken ill, which was true. I was moved there so I could help Helen. Nobody knew about the cancer at first, except me. Then after the surgery in Inverness, she became worse. She was dying.

'Mike had called saying he was coming up. I played her answering machine and I knew I couldn't let him talk to her. She was drugged up and God knows what she would have said to him. When I knew he was due to arrive, I told the doctor that Helen had requested the last rites. You don't have to be on death's doorstep to get them, but I knew Helen was close to dying. So I gave her the last rites and then put a pillow over her face. I knew they wouldn't do a postmortem because they were expecting her to go any time.'

O'Brian looked at the mirror. 'That's right, Mike, I murdered our mother. Then I came down here and killed your brother Hugh. Walter too. Phil's sons. You were going to get it too, so I would be the only one left alive.'

'You were the one who was spotted in your mother's house by the neighbour, weren't you?' Harry said.

'I was. She saw me from a distance though, or else she would have known it was me. She thought it was Helen's brother. I was working and living in Brora, just five minutes up the road, so it was easy for me to get in.'

'And you wrote the journal.'

'I did. I wanted to make Mike think our father was a killer. I hid it in Helen's car. I also stole the laptop, but I didn't realise at the time it was an old one.'

'We found the photos on the new one,' Stewart said. 'And if you're going to make up a lie about something, make sure it can't be checked out afterwards. Mike said you went and got Helen's house keys from the hospital and gave them to him. One phone call to the hospital confirmed that you didn't get them there. You had them all the time, didn't you?'

'Correct again. And I took the model bus he was looking for. It was special to Mike, so it had to go. I put it in the rubbish bin.'

'You had it all figured out, didn't you?' Stewart said.

'I did actually.' O'Brian beamed a smile at them. 'I was far cleverer than Detective Phil ever was.'

'Really?' Harry said.

'Really. And way more intelligent than Helen had ever been.'

'They were clever enough to keep their other child a secret from you.'

O'Brian suddenly sat forward. 'What? You're lying.'

Harry smiled. 'No, I'm not. You didn't know about her. But when Helen talked to Mike about keeping a journal, she knew her handwriting was awful. Richard told Mike this too; her handwriting was a chicken scrawl. That's why she typed it on her new laptop and kept it in cloud storage. Mike read it and showed us. I've never met your sister, but Mike has. Just recently. And so have you, apparently.'

O'Brian smiled. 'Nah. My mother wouldn't have

had another child without telling me. I would have known if she was pregnant.'

'This wasn't after she had you, Dan; this was *before.*'

'I don't believe you. She had another boy after Mike and he died. Then she had me. I know she was still seeing Phil Nichol, and they had me in nineteen seventy-three. She didn't have any more children.'

Stewart looked at him. 'She did. October first, nineteen seventy. "Eileen" it says on her birth certificate. But of course her adoptive parents changed that, and her name changed when she got married. Her husband died, so it was just her because she had no kids. She moved up to Golspie to be near her mum. I believe you met her. Mike did too. Her original name was Eileen, but you know her as Maggie. Maggie Quinn. I believe she helped you box up Helen's things. Her mother's things.'

The evil that was sitting like a small fire kindling away suddenly became a roaring inferno. 'No! You lying fuckers!' O'Brian said, jumping to his feet.

The uniform ran forward and tackled him while others rushed into the room, piling onto the raging priest. They grabbed him and started hauling him out.

'So you see, even if you'd killed Mike, you

wouldn't have been the only offspring left. You still have a sister.'

'Bastards!' O'Brian replied. Then he was dragged away, kicking and screaming.

Holland walked in. 'Christ, he's a nutcase.'

'He certainly is,' Stewart said, making sure the recording was switched off. 'I'm glad I booted his fucking baws for him.'

'Does it not make you feel bad that you kicked a priest?' Harry asked.

'How long have you known me, Harry, son?' Stewart laughed. 'Good job, Mike. Now you can enjoy your retirement in peace when it comes.'

'I don't think my mind will be at peace for a long time, sir. But at least I have a sister I can go and spend time with.'

'There's always that,' Harry said. He reminded himself to call his own brother and sister soon.

THIRTY-EIGHT

'Miles Tate got the keys to his flat today,' Kim Miller said. She and her husband were sitting on the couch, watching some TV.

'Did he now?' Frank Miller replied.

'Yes. And he invited us over for a glass of wine to celebrate.'

Miller looked over at her. 'You have got to be kidding me. I couldn't be more uninterested.' He looked back at the TV.

'Come on, the night's young. Jack and Samantha are just along the corridor. She said they're staying in tonight and they're willing to babysit.'

'You've already asked them then? You were planning on going, so you went behind my back and then waited until I was comfortable watching some TV before pouncing on me with the idea.'

'Oh, don't be like that. It's just a little impromptu housewarming party.'

Miller sighed. 'I'm knackered. It's a weekday. I just want to stay in.'

Kim stood up and looked at him, then shook her head. She thought that maybe she should have gone for a drink with Miles when he had asked her. At least that would have been a little bit more exciting than whatever this was that she and her husband had going on.

She left the living room and went through to the bedroom where the girls were playing. 'Mummy's going out. She won't be long, okay?'

'Is Daddy staying in?' Emma asked.

'Yes, honey, he's staying in with you. I won't be long.'

She kissed them and opened the closet in the hallway and pulled out her jacket, before going back to the living room. Miller looked up when he saw she had her jacket on.

'You're going then?' he said to her.

'Yes. And you could come along too. Please come. Some people from my work are going. My dad will be there.'

'Kim, I'm knackered. This was a tough case, okay? Not made any easier by your department not filling us in with all the details.'

'You know I can't discuss certain things with you. Why are you being like that?'

'But you can discuss them with Superman Miles.'

Kim shook her head. 'He works in the department. You're being ridiculous now, Frank. What's got into you anyway?'

'Nothing. You're not the only one with a tough job.'

'Don't wait up,' she said, leaving the living room.

Downstairs, her father was waiting in the Range Rover, driving himself for a change.

She got in the passenger seat.

'Frank not coming?' McGovern asked her.

She shook her head. 'No, he's being stubborn.'

'Did he tell you where he was the other night?' McGovern asked as he drove away down the North Bridge.

'No, he says he got drunk and can't remember. He stayed at a friend's house.'

McGovern stopped at the traffic lights. 'He still obsessed with his first wife?'

Kim looked at her father. 'Yes he is.'

'You can't blame the man.'

'I don't blame him. But our relationship is on the way out.'

McGovern smiled. 'It lasted longer than what we had anticipated.'

They drove the rest of the way in silence.

After they parked, they walked to the front door of Tate's building. She took the piece of paper out of her pocket and read the words again.

We know where you are.

She crumpled the paper up and shoved it back in her pocket.